CAT ATTACK!

Other Avon Camelot Books by
Tim Schoch

CREEPS
FLASH FRY, PRIVATE EYE
SUMMER CAMP CREEPS

TIM SCHOCH grew up in New Jersey and gradu-
ated from the University of Tampa with a degree in
Drama. He has been a full-time actor and singer
and currently works for a major New York City
publisher. His first three Avon Camelot novels for
young readers were *Creeps, Summer Camp Creeps,*
and *Flash Fry, Private Eye.* He has also written
three mysteries for adults, many pieces of humor,
more than 250 songs, and a musical comedy act,
which he has performed with his partner, actor
Jerry Winsett. Tim thanks all the great kids who
have sent him letters about his books, and he will
happily answer anyone who writes him in care of
Avon Books. Tim lives with his wife, Wendy
McCurdy, and their son, Alexander, in New Jersey.

CAT ATTACK!

TIM SCHOCH

Pictures by Neal McPheeters

AN AVON  CAMELOT BOOK

CAT ATTACK! is an original publication of Avon Books. This work has never before appeared in book form.

AVON BOOKS
A division of
The Hearst Corporation
105 Madison Avenue
New York, New York 10016

First Avon Camelot Printing: December 1988

CAMELOT TRADEMARK REG. U.S. PAT. OFF. AND IN OTHER COUNTRIES, MARCA REGISTRADA, HECHO EN U.S.A.

Printed in the U.S.A.

OPM   10   9   8   7   6   5   4   3   2   1

To my loving wife, Wendy,
and our beautiful baby son, Alexander

One: A Frightening Furry Morning

I woke up with a bark. Actually, I think I barked first, then woke myself up. Dogs do that. I'm a dog, a bulldog. Scratch is my name—Scratch, Private Nose. I'm in the detective business with a kid named Flash Fry, Private Eye. Right now Flash was sound asleep. Me, I was curled up at his feet— under the covers where it's warm.

I poked my handsome head out and saw brilliant golden sunshine slashing down to the floor. I barked again, this time trying to wake up Flash. It didn't work. I flipped off the covers, raised my back leg, and scratched my ear like crazy, making the bed shake like it was traveling down a bumpy road. Flash still didn't wake up. I stood, walked up beside him, and let his face have it with my wide, wet tongue.

"Huh? What? Yuk!"

1

That woke him up. I leapt off the bed, stretched, and was ready for action.

"Where am I? Who am I? What am I? What day is this? Awk!" Flash flopped back down onto his pillow.

It was the last Saturday morning in July. About eight-fifteen. I was ready for breakfast, but Flash was fading out again. I jumped up on the bed, barked, drooled, then lapped at his ear. That did it.

"Yuk, Scratch! Will you cut it out? Okay, okay! I'm up, I'm up! Geesh!"

Fifteen minutes later Flash Fry was dressed. Flash dresses kind of normal for a kid his age, except for one thing. He wears this big 1940s-type hat like the detectives in those old black-and-white movies wear. Flash's hat is grass green. He has to stick an entire *TV Guide* inside the brim to make it fit. He thinks he's cool.

Me, I don't need a hat. I'm cool already. I was also very hungry. I wagged my stubby tail and pranced around in a circle, hoping Flash would get the message. He did.

"Okay, Scratch, let's go! Breakfast time! But first..." Flash paused at the top of the stairs and sniffed the air. "Let's see what my skilled detective nose tells me this morning. Hmmmmm. Something is cooking. Smells like...toast. Lots of toast. So that means eggs. But what's that other smell in the air? It smells like wood—firewood! I'll bet Dad got a shipment of firewood for the winter. Come on, let's go down and see!"

Firewood—in July?

Downstairs in the kitchen, Flash's mother had just served Flash's dad pancakes and was mixing pancake batter for Flash's breakfast. There went Flash's toast theory.

Naturally, my nose knew what they were eating. Pancakes and maple syrup. Maybe some sausage, too, soaked in syrup. Yummmm. But would I get those goodies? Nope. I'd be led down to the basement, where Flash would open a cold can of some revolting dog food and flop it into my plastic bowl. Dogs get no respect.

"Morning," said Flash's mom. "Half hour till baseball practice."

"Morning," said Flash. "Thanks."

"Morning, sport," said Flash's dad, peeking around the corner of his newspaper.

"Morning, Dad."

"I put Scratch's food down already," his dad said. "But I forgot to check his water. And be careful down in the basement because I've been cutting some wood for that picnic table I'm making."

Wood. Flash's father was cutting wood. No, he hadn't ordered firewood in July. Flash had better train his nose a little more.

"Okay, Dad. Come on, Scratch, let's go downstairs and eat!" Flash said this like we were both going to a Taco Bell or something. I took a long last sniff of the pancakes and followed Flash down into the basement.

"Well," said Flash, "at least I was close on the wood."

Geesh.

As soon as Flash opened the basement door, my nose went crazy. *"WOOFFTT!"* I sneezed. Zillions of tiny bits of sawdust were hovering in the air like a gnat rally. Immediately my eyes started watering and my nose clogged up—but not before I smelled

3

something else. What I smelled was big trouble. I growled.

"What's wrong, Scratch?" Flash asked.

I hate it when Flash asks me questions. What's he want me to do, talk? Write him a note? I just shook my head and led the way down into the basement.

"*AH-CHOO!*" Flash sneezed. Flash's nose knew what was down there, even if his brain didn't. "*AH-CHOO-CHOO!*"

I sat at the bottom of the stairs and waited for Flash to see what I saw. Finally, he did.

"Cats!" he whispered, covering up his mouth and nose. "*AH-AH...CHOO!*"

Three cats were calmly wandering around in the basement. There was a chubby orange cat with yellow stripes, a black one with a white nose, and a brown one with black feet. If my nose hadn't been all stuffed up by the sawdust, maybe I could have smelled where they came from. I wandered over near the basement window and breathed some of the fresh air that was dropping in.

"*AH-AH-CHOO!*"

And, oh yes: Flash is allergic to cats.

"Cats!" he said again. "Oh, no." He looked up to the basement window. "The window is open! Dad must have left it open. Oh, no. *AH-AH-CHOO—DARN!* Got to get rid of them, Scratch. I can't stand having them around—I have to work down here!"

See, part of the basement is Flash's office. His desk is down there, his chair, and his old-time red Coke machine that Flash stocks with grape soda, his favorite kind. Everything was now covered with sheets of plastic that were dusted with sawdust from his father's sawing.

4

I thought about chasing the cats, but that would have stirred everything up and made things even messier. Besides, one of the cats smiled at me. And when it smiled, I got a whiff of something else: dog food. I checked my bowl on the floor. Yup, empty. The furry things ate my food!

Flash took a deep breath, ran up the steps leading to the bulkhead, flung open the doors, ran back downstairs, managed to grab all three cats at once, then ran up the stairs and outside, where he exhaled and caught another breath. I followed, laughing silently. The air outside was clean and great.

The cats were twisting and clawing all over him, but Flash's grip was tight as he bolted straight through the backyard and into the woods. I paused to lift my leg carefully against one of the thorny rosebushes, then caught up with Flash, snapping at a couple of pesky flies on my way. It was a beautiful blue-sky morning.

Flash ran down the zigzagging path that, if you followed it all the way, led to the pond where a kid named Brick Glick had a kind of hideout where he captured frogs and watched them eat green bugs that he fed them. But Flash stopped by a huge tree and set the cats down. They frantically scurried away, bumping into one another, heading for the thickest bushes they could find.

"CHOO! AH-CHOO!" Flash said, brushing off his shirt and jeans as we headed back to the house.

I took a few moments to roll in some nice dewy weeds and rip off a mouthful of grass to chew. Flash yelled at me to stop those things and get inside. Poor boy. He just doesn't know how to enjoy life. If anybody needed a good roll in the weeds it was Flash.

Back in the basement Flash now saw what I had seen.

"Hey! The cats must have eaten your food! I know because Dad just told me he put your food out. Yeah. The cats saw the open window, smelled the food, and just jumped inside and ate it. They sure must have been hungry."

Yeah, I thought, like me.

"Come on, Scratch! Now I've got to hurry if I want to eat breakfast and make baseball practice!" Flash headed for the kitchen.

I trotted beside him. Flash couldn't afford to miss practice. His team was playing their biggest rival tomorrow, and they needed all the practice they could get.

"What took you so long?" asked Flash's mom as we came back into the kitchen.

"Oh," said Flash, "three cats jumped into the basement and were running all around Dad's new table, so I had to chase them and catch them and throw them outside. Now I have to feed Scratch again because they ate his food, too."

Flash's father laughed. "What a story! You sure they were just cats? No elephants or anything?"

Flash shrugged and smiled while he fed me some gray Beef-O dog food. I wolfed it down, and Flash gave me his syrupy plate to lick off, which was great. Then he got up to leave.

"Practice hard," said his mom. "Dad and I want to see a victory tomorrow!"

Flash chuckled. "Then you'd better tune in the Mets on TV. Bye."

Flash grabbed his hat, bat, and glove, and we headed off for the baseball field in the park.

Two: Practice Makes Purr-fect

On our walk through the sunshine to the ballpark, Flash tossed sticks up ahead of him and I brought them back. He loves to play these kinds of games because he thinks he's got me trained to go fetch the stick. Ha. What he doesn't know is that I've got *him* trained to *throw* the sticks. All I have to do is jump around in front of him when we're walking along and, sure enough, he'll bend down, pick up a stick, and toss it. He's a very loyal and faithful boy.

Flash's summer baseball team was called the Pink Bunny Lasers, named after the store that gave the team money to buy uniforms and equipment, Pink Bunny Pet Store. The Pink Bunny Lasers were not thrilled with their pink-and-white uniforms. They also weren't proud of the fact that they'd lost eleven games and won none. The final game of the season was tomorrow, and they were

playing the toughest, best team in the whole summer league, the Lucky Laundry Tornadoes. The
Lucky Laundry Tornadoes had brilliant blue-and-
yellow uniforms and had won eleven games and lost
none.

Flash's Pink Bunny Lasers knew they were going
to be mutilated tomorrow afternoon.

Flash's whole team was sitting on the bench in
their pink baseball caps when Flash arrived in his
pink baseball cap.

"You are late, Mr. Fry," said the coach of the Pink
Bunny Lasers, Mr. Slith. He was a tall, skinny man
with the biggest and thickest glasses a guy could
wear without crushing his nose.

"Sorry, Mr. Slith," said Flash, sitting with the
rest of his teammates.

"Apology accepted," said Mr. Slith.

"Mr. Slith thure ith a nith guy," said Pete Hurst-
wurst, a practical joker and one of Flash's good buddies.

"Please, please, please," groaned Mr. Slith. *"Must
you always make fun of my name? Please don't do it
anymore."

"I promith," said Pete.

We all broke up.

"Quiet!" Mr. Slith shouted. "Now, team, this is a
very important practice for us. Extremely important. We play the number one team tomorrow."

"We know, we know," said Brick Glick, a good left
fielder but a real complainer. He used to think he
was a great magician, but now he thinks he's a
great baseball player. He also doesn't like dogs. "So
why bother? The only half-decent pitcher we had,
Max, moved away. And who do we get to replace
him? Some new girl named Rosie—a *girl!* I'll tell

8

you, we've lost all our games and we'll lose to the Tornadoes, too. They'll blow us away. It's embarrassing."

The rest of the team slumped down and mumbled their agreement. Flash's team didn't have a lot of spirit. They had had it knocked out of them by losing the last eleven games—for good reason, too: they stink. Sorry, but true. I ought to know. I love baseball and watch it all the time on TV. I know more about baseball than any dog I know, and more than most humans. Believe me, Flash's team stinks. But even stinky teams can win once in a while if they keep their spirit. Especially if they have a secret weapon.

"Stop that kind of talk, will you?" whined Mr. Slith. "Besides, are all you kids blind or something? Rosie is a great pitcher. She's our secret weapon. You saw her at practice last Thursday. That girl can hurl!"

"Oh, great, now Mr. Slith is rhyming," said Pete.

"We have to believe in ourselves," Mr. Slith continued. "We have to rally for one final effort and crush the opposition when they least expect it."

"You mean we can jump them after the game and rumble?" said chunky Curtis Melloner, the second baseman.

"No, no, Curtis, you know that is not what I meant," said Mr. Slith. *"Please,* team, let's get serious! Come on now, take the field and let's practice like we've never practiced before."

"You mean good?" said Brick Glick.

"On the field!" screamed Mr. Slith.

The Pink Bunny Lasers kind of shuffled out onto the field. Even George Numper, the catcher, was extra quiet. George was the quietest kid in the world. We wouldn't even know George was there if we didn't see him. Mr. Slith grabbed the bat and began to hit ground balls.

First he hit one to Flash at first base. The ball hit Flash's foot, bounced up, hit him in the chest and fell into his glove, and Flash touched first. He grinned.

"Great catch!" said Mr. Slith.

I shook my head and found some shade to settle into. Even if Rosie McRoy was Dwight Gooden, they wouldn't have a chance.

Curtis caught the grounder to second, but he couldn't get it out of his glove. He had to take his glove off and pry the ball out.

"Good thing the ball didn't hit your big gut," called Brick from center field. "You would have lost it!"

Mr. Slith hit a quick bouncer to Brenda Zeek, the blond shortstop. She snagged it cleanly. Very good.

Pete Hurthwurst at third base saw the ball screaming toward him and ducked. Marybeth, Pete's sister, picked it up in left field and threw it in.

"Good play, Marybeth," shouted Mr. Slith.

Then he hit a really high, long fly ball to Brick Glick in center field. Brick turned and tore off, angled under the ball, caught it cleanly, and threw a rocket back in to Mr. Slith at home. "Excellent!" called Mr. Slith.

"I'm too good for this stinking team," said Brick. "It's embarrassing. Maybe I ought to drop a few just so I can fit in."

"Stop bragging, Brick," said Flash. "If you used your mouth, you'd catch twice as many balls."

Everybody laughed but Brick.

"Go on, laugh," said Brick. "But if I can't save this team with my superior baseball talents, no girl is going to either."

Gene Reese, the cleanest and neatest kid in town, was in right field. He let a slow grounder go between his legs. He threw the ball in and it didn't even reach Flash at first.

"We're doomed," Brick said, over and over again. "Maybe the Tornadoes will be laughing so hard they'll miss a few balls and we can score some funny runs."

Me, I wished Brick wouldn't be so hard on the rest of the team. Sure, he was a pretty good ball player, but he wasn't great. If he was on a really good team, he might end up being the worst player. But try to tell that to big-headed Brick.

Finally, the last of the Pink Bunny Lasers arrived at practice. Rosie McRoy walked up with her bushy red hair sticking out from the edges of her pink Pink Bunny baseball cap. She looked cute, but she wasn't smiling.

"Well," said Mr. Slith, "and where have you been, young lady? Do you know you are one half hour late? Do you know that tomorrow we play the Lucky Laundry Tornadoes, and you are our secret weapon, and... Hey, now, what's wrong?"

Rosie leaned against the backstop and started crying. A flood of tears rolled down her freckled cheeks. We all ran in to see what was wrong.

"Rosie, what's the matter?" Brenda asked.

"Where's your glove?" asked Curtis.

"All right, now, just back off everybody, just back off," said Mr. Slith. "I'm the coach here. I'll find out what's wrong."

"Yeth, thir!" said Pete.

11

"So, Rosie," said Mr. Slith, "what's wrong?"

Rosie tried to speak but only burst into a new round of sobbing. I licked Rosie's hand. She patted my head and went on crying.

"I think she just realized who we're playing tomorrow," said Brick. "In fact, I think I might start crying, too."

"Will you stop that kind of talk," said Brenda. "We might win the game, you know."

"Yeah, and the sky might turn to chocolate ice cream, too," said Brick.

"Knock it off, Brick," said Flash.

"Knock off your head?" asked Brick. "Anytime."

"Rosie?" said Mr. Slith.

"I... I'm sorry!" said Rosie.

"Hey, you weren't *that* late to practice," said Mr. Slith.

"I-It's not that," she said. "It's... well... something horrible has happened."

"Oh, for crying out loud," said Brick. "Do we have to guess for a million years, or what? Come on, what's bugging you?"

Rosie lifted her swollen face to us. "The... The Three Stooges are gone!"

We all looked at each other and shrugged.

"Don't worry," Pete said, "they're on reruns."

"No, not them," Rosie said. "My three cats. My *mother's* three cats. The cats I was supposed to be taking care of. They're gone. When I let them out of the house this morning, they ran away. We just moved here and the neighborhood is still strange to them. They'll never find their way back home. Mom yelled and screamed at me all morning. I looked and looked for them but couldn't find them, and when I got back Mom screamed at me some more. It was horrible. Oh, what am I going to do?" And she burst out crying again.

Gene looked at the rest of us. "She calls her cats The Three Stooges?"

Rosie nodded "yes."

Brenda said, "Rosie's mother named them Curly, Larry, and Moe. So, they're The Three Stooges."

"They're kind of cute," Rosie said, "but they can be a big pain. And"—she started crying again—"that's not the worst thing of all!"

"I think we'd better ask her what, or we'll be here all day," said Brick.

"What, Rosie?" asked Mr. Slith.

"I-I c-can't p-play any more b-baseball until the c-cats are found."

"What!" Flash said.

"But...but...but," said Mr. Slith.

"You're our best pitcher," said Gene.

"You're our *only* pitcher," said Flash.

"We can't lose you!" said Brenda.

"That's right," said Marybeth. "We can't win without you."

"We won't win at all," said Brick. "We'll have to forfeit the game because we'll be a player short. I don't know which is more embarrassing: losing with Rosie, or having to forfeit without her. Why did I have to be stuck with a team that can't play? Why me?"

"Shut up, Brick!" Mr. Slith shrieked. He had taken off his hat and was rubbing his thin-haired head. He was nearly hysterical. "What'll we do now? Where do we get another player? Where do we get another pitcher? What an awful thing to happen before the big game. Oh, my. Gee whiz."

"Alllll right, everybody, stand back," Flash said.

13

"There's a detective on the scene who needs some facts."

"Really? Where is he?" Pete joked. Everybody laughed except Brick, who snorted.

"Now," Flash said, squatting down beside Rosie. "If I find your cats, you can play, right? Right. So, I'm going to find your cats. What do they look like?"

"Well," Rosie said, "Curly is orange with yellow stripes. Larry is black with a cute white nose. And Moe is brown with black shoes. I mean black feet."

"I see, I see," Flash said, thinking.

Oh, no. I gulped and started to whine.

Flash took a little more time than I had, but soon he gulped and started to whine, too.

"Flash, you okay?" asked Curtis. "You look kind of pale."

"I...I..." Flash said.

Oh, this is going to be bad, I thought. I could only watch with one eye.

"Flash?" Rosie asked. "Does it have something to do with my lost cats?"

"I...I..." Flash said again.

"Out with it, Fry," Brick said. "We don't have all day."

So Flash had to tell them.

"See, well, I, um, it's that..." Flash said.

"What are you talking about?" Rosie said.

"I...well, I saw your cats. They were in the woods behind my house."

"They were?" Rosie asked hopefully. "I wonder what they were doing there."

"I, um, sort of put them there," Flash said.

"You what!"

Then Flash spilled all the beans. "I guess they came over because of Scratch's food. Our basement

14

window was open, so they hopped in and ate the food. I had to get the cats out of my house. Cats make me sneeze. I didn't realize they were yours, so I just grabbed them and chucked them way out in the woods behind my house, near the pond. I feel awful."

"Oh, Flash!" Rosie said.

"Oh, no!" said Curtis.

"Oh, terrific!" said Marybeth.

"Oh, arrrggghh!" said Flash.

Even quiet George almost said something.

"He had Rosie's cats in his arms, and he threw The Three Stooges in the woods!" screeched Brick, laughing. "What a great detective, huh? Now there's a *fourth* stooge!"

"Shut up, Brick," Flash said. "I've got to think. Rosie, are you sure your cats haven't gone home?"

"I'm sure," she said. "They're probably lost out there...somewhere."

"Well, well," said Mr. Slith, "it looks like we have us a problem. We are short a player for the big game tomorrow."

"Unless I find the cats!" said Flash.

"I really hope you do," said Mr. Slith. "In fact, let's think positively. Let us all assume that Flash will find the cats and Rosie will be able to play. Let's have some batting practice. Everyone, take your positions. Rosie, I can't risk you hurting your arm, so you warm up your arm on the side with George. Gene, you throw to the batters, and Brick, you're up first. I'll catch. Hustle, hustle!"

They did what Mr. Slith said. Brick grabbed a metal bat and stood up at the plate like a big shot. Me, I grabbed some shade under the bench.

Gene threw a couple of slow pitches to warm up.

16

He had no follow-through or power. Now, Brick was ready, waving his bat around and smiling. Gene took a big windup and threw the ball as hard as he could. Immediately, he held his arm and screamed, "It *hurts*, it really *hurts!*"

Mr. Slith sighed and shook his head. "Gene, right field. Flash, you pitch."

Flash stood up on the pitcher's mound. If Flash didn't spend so much time being a detective, he might make a fairly good baseball player. Anyway, lately he'd been throwing in his backyard with me, practicing curve balls and throwing pop-ups to me. I'm a great catcher, I never miss a pop-up. Someday, maybe I'll get a chance to really play.

"Let's go, Flash," said Brick. "I'll blast one over the fence off you."

Flash didn't say anything. He bent over and made believe he was getting a sign from the catcher. He nodded. Brick rolled his eyes. Flash slowly straightened up, took a nice slow windup, then hurled the ball toward the plate. The ball was heading right toward Brick's hands. Brick stepped back, and the ball suddenly curved and went right over the plate.

"Strike one!" said Mr. Slith, giggling.

"A curve ball!" whispered Curtis to Marybeth.

"I'll get you this time!" said Brick, hammering the bat on the plate.

Flash got his sign, wound up, then chucked the ball. Brick took a big swing but missed the ball completely.

"Strike two!" said Mr. Slith.

"*Another* curve ball," said Curtis.

"I think we might have found a relief pitcher," said Mr. Slith.

17

"Yeah," said Brick, "comic relief."

Flash was getting really cocky now. His head was bobbing and he spat into his glove and rubbed it in. Then he spat toward the ground but it landed on his sneaker.

"Come on, Fry!" Brick was yelling. "No creep like you is going to strike me out!"

Flash got his sign again and went into his windup. He fired the ball and it was soaring right toward Brick's hands. Brick didn't move. He just stood there, waiting for the curve to break over the plate. It didn't break—it nailed him on the fists.

"Yeeow!" Brick screamed, dropping the bat, hopping around, and shaking his left hand.

"No curve that time," Curtis whispered.

"I'll get you for that!" Brick screamed at Flash.

"I'm sorry, Brick, really, I really am," Flash said.

"Am I the only one on this lousy team who can throw a baseball?" asked Brick.

"Rosie can," said Brenda.

"We have to find her cats," Flash said. "It's our only hope. If we find her cats we get Rosie back."

"Right!" Pete said.

Mr. Slith sat on the bench with his head in his hands. "Practice over. See you at the game tomorrow."

Instead of leaving, the team ran over to Rosie again. Everybody except Brick.

"I'm going home," Brick growled. "I've gotta soak this hand in ice water."

"Come on, Brick, it's not that bad," said Flash. "I only grazed you. Besides, don't you want to help us find the cats?"

18

"No," said Brick. "You losers will never find them anyway. Besides, who cares whether Rosie can play or not. We're better off if we forfeit the game! Just give up and tell them they won without playing!"

For once, Mr. Slith got mad. "I don't want to hear that kind of talk anymore, Brick. You be here for the game tomorrow, and don't be late!"

"Okay, okay," said Brick. And he hopped on his bike and rode off.

"Flash, do you think my cats are still in the woods?" Rosie asked.

"Maybe they're back at your house already, Rosie," Curtis said.

"Or maybe they're in the pond," said Marybeth.

"Great. Thanks, Marybeth," said Rosie.

"I'll go look for them right now," Flash said, standing. "Maybe Scratch and I can sniff them out."

"Maybe we all should help," Rosie said.

"Good idea!" Flash said. "Okay, everybody, we have until one o'clock tomorrow afternoon to find those cats. Rosie, you check to see if the cats have gone home. The rest of you drop your equipment off at your houses and meet at my house in fifteen minutes!"

I trotted beside Flash as he raced home. He was mumbling to himself. "Jerk. Airhead. Wood brain! How could I be so dumb? Why didn't I try to find the owners of the cats instead of chucking them in the woods? What a mess. The way those cats took off into the woods, we'll never find them. Never. Maybe I should just stay there and live in the woods for the rest of my life. I lost Rosie's cats, Rosie's mother will kill her, even if we find a ninth player we'll still

19

lose the big game, everybody will hate me, and I'll lose all my friends. Airhead! Cement brain!"

When we got home, some more bad news was waiting for poor Flash.

Three: On the Trail of Three Tails

As soon as we got home, Flash took off his pink baseball cap and put on his grass-green gangster hat. We ran into Flash's father in the backyard on the way to the woods. He had the back basement door and the window open, sweeping sawdust outside.

"You can't use your basement office for a while, Flash," said his father.

"Why?" Flash asked.

"I'm going to be putting wood stain on the picnic table and I don't want you investigating all over down there and stirring up sawdust."

"But, Dad!"

"Sorry, Flash. And that goes for Scratch, too. I don't want dog hair embedded in the picnic table."

"Okay, Dad," Flash said. "Come on, Scratch."

Once outside, Flash started mumbling. "Great.

How can a professional detective run a business without an office?"

I looked up at him and hung my tongue out to show I was listening.

"Well," he said, "I guess I'll just have to use my brain for an office."

Small office, I thought.

Just then the rest of the team hurried into the backyard.

"Hi, Flash!" said Pete.

"Were the cats at Rosie's house?" Flash asked.

One look at Rosie's sad face told everybody the cats were not there.

"What now?" asked Brenda.

"Now, we have to be organized," Flash said. "Scratch and I will backtrack our path of this morning. But we have to cover the whole woods in case the cats wandered."

"So, why don't we split up?" Curtis asked.

Flash shot him a glare. "Curtis, I'm the detective around here. I'll tell you what to do."

"Fine, fine," said Curtis.

"We'll split up," Flash said. "Curtis, you and Gene head off to the left. Pete, you and Marybeth head off to the right."

With a wave, the four kids took off into the woods.

"Flash, do you think there is any hope of finding them?" Rosie asked.

"Rosie," Flash said, "as long as I'm on the case, there's always hope."

Oh, geez! Stuck up, isn't he?"

"So, Rosie, you and Brenda take that path to the right, there. It goes all the way around the pond in the woods. Scratch and I will take the path to the left, the one we took this morning."

"Thanks, Flash," Rosie said. "You sure are a good friend for helping out. All of you guys are good friends."

"It's nothing," Flash said, blushing. "Good luck."

Rosie and Brenda waved, then disappeared into the foliage.

I grabbed a mouthful of grass to chew, then put my nose to the path and soon picked up the trail of the three cats. Now I recognized their scent from having sniffed traces of it on Rosie. If my super nose hadn't been clogged up with sawdust this morning, we might not have been in this mess right now. But was that my fault? Nope.

"Smell them, boy? Huh?"

Since I couldn't answer him—and if I could, he'd scream—I just wagged my adorable stubby tail and moved a little faster down the path. Soon we arrived at the place where Flash had dropped off the cats this morning. I crashed into the bushes, smelling everything, with Flash right behind me. I sniffed a strange red bug that smelled like a root. I sniffed some squirrel droppings, a few rotten berries, a mouldering dead mouse, the thin trail of a snake, ant tracks, and the footprints of The Three Stooges. Flash followed behind me as best he could, whacking himself in the face with branches and stumbling over rocks. He held his nose as we hiked past the dead mouse.

Soon we were back on the path again. I stopped.

"What's wrong, boy? Huh?"

I'd stopped because I lost the scent of the cats. Lots of kids and their dogs come down this path toward the pond. Everybody likes to hack around at

23

the pond. With all the kid and dog footprints around there, and with all those footprints smelling like everywhere else they'd been and everything else they'd stepped in, I couldn't smell a single cat. I wandered around, getting my nose all dirty and filled with soggy grass and stuff, but I'd lost the trail. I had no idea where the cats had gone.

Flash soon caught on and sat on a rock.

"Now what? Think, think. Hmmmm."

Sometimes, Flash takes a little bit of time to think things out. I always have to be patient. I wandered over to a little stream and took a few laps of the trickling water. A crawfish made a grab for my nose, but he missed. I chuckled at it. Then I went back beside Flash, dug a long, shallow hole, and nuzzled my belly down into the cool dirt. Ahhhh.

"I've got it!" Flash said. "I've got to treat this case like I would any other case. I have to stick to the techniques that made me the famous detective that I am today. We have to do some legwork, Scratch. Maybe someone around the neighborhood has seen the cats. Come on, let's ask some questions."

So, I spent the next half hour or so following Flash up and down our street, going to all the houses along the woods and asking the neighbors if they'd seen The Three Stooges this morning. No one had.

"Darn," Flash said.

When we got back home, the rest of the team was waiting. They were all slumped around Flash's front steps. No one had had any luck.

"We're doomed," Gene said. "Here we are looking for cats. If we don't find them, we have to forfeit the game. If we do find them, we play ball. If we play ball, we lose."

"Oh, shut up, Gene," Brenda said. "You're beginning to sound like Brick Glick."

"But the Tornadoes are undefeated! And we are nothing *but* defeated," Gene said.

"But we *could* win," said Rosie. "It's happened before, teams coming out of last place to win it all, the last-place team killing the first-place team. It could happen to us, too."

Gene shook his head. "Rosie, you're new. You haven't been here all season to see how bad we really are."

Everyone sighed at the same time.

"I'd better get back on the case now," Flash said. "If I need anybody's help, I'll call. And if you have any ideas, call me or just get going."

"Do you have a plan?" Pete asked Flash.

"Do I have a plan?" Flash said. "You're asking if Flash Fry, Private Eye, has a plan?"

"Yeah, I am," Pete said.

"Sort of," Flash said. "I'll let you know later."

They said good-bye to one another, and the team left.

We sat there for a minute, then we heard a whistle from down the street. We looked up, and there was Brick Glick riding his bike across the street. He was shaking his fist at Flash. Flash shook his fist back and went inside.

Four: A Cat Plan

Last night it had rained, and I noticed that clouds were moving slowly overhead again. My dog-sense told me that it would rain again tonight. I was never wrong.

Flash and I had moved up onto the large front porch of his house. Flash was sitting on a bright red folding chair. In front of him was a yellow plastic TV tray with pictures of little tiny flowers all over it. He sat there with his 1940s green hat trying to be a cool detective, but he really did look silly.

Me, I missed the nice cool concrete floor of the basement and hoped Flash's dad would finish that table fast.

"How can I even think under these conditions?" Flash asked.

He got up and started to pace the porch. His

sneakers squeaked loudly on the painted wooden floorboards.

"How can I figure out what is the best thing to do first?" He paced some more. Then he stopped. "Hmmm. Maybe. Just maybe we could—I've got to think this out."

Like I said, thinking sometimes takes Flash a little while. I lay there with my chin on my paws, watching a small red spider climb up the porch wall then fall. Then I got to thinking about baseball and how much I'd really like to go out back and have a catch with Flash. A kid can play catch with himself, but it's awful hard for a dog. Flash and I used to play catch all the time, but just when I had been starting to get really good, he went off on a case and the practicing stopped. The spider started climbing the wall again. Oh, well.

"Yeah! It might just work!" Flash said. "Come on, Scratch, I have to talk with Rosie again."

Well, I had nothing else to do, so why not?

I followed Flash outside and into the garage, where he stopped and just stood in front of his beat-up bike.

"Slugs. I forgot to fix the flat on my bike. Well, no time now. Let's move out, Scratch."

Rosie's house was at the far end of our development, and Flash hustled along the sidewalk at a pretty good pace. For me, the pace was slow, but I panted to make him believe he was moving fast. I did get thirsty, though, and I soon spotted a big mud puddle in the gutter. I stopped to take a few laps. Suddenly Flash's fingers were around my collar, dragging me away.

"Yuk! Dirty water, Scratch! Yuk!" he scolded.

I wanted to tell him that the junk in the water

wasn't any worse than some of the things they put into the soda he drinks, but, of course, I couldn't. What humans don't realize is that we dogs smell things before we eat them. If it smells really bad, dogs won't eat it. If it smells good, we do—no matter what it is. I've been known to eat a good-smelling bug or two. They're great, but not too filling. Crunchy, too.

"Now stay away from those awful puddles, understand?" he asked.

Boy, I wished I could answer him, but when I tried all that came out of my chops was a kind of whine. I just can't get my mouth and brain to speak English. I think in English, but it doesn't make any sense when it comes out of my mouth. Maybe someday I'll figure it out and suddenly start yakking away. I can't wait to see Flash's face when I do!

So, I trotted along beside Flash, snapping at bugs and sniffing here and there, as we continued on to Rosie's house. But we never made it there, mainly because we found Rosie first. She was sitting on the curb with her best friend, Brenda. What interested me most was that right beside Brenda was her huge Great Dane, Kong, who was one of my best buddies. So while Flash talked to Rosie and Brenda, I talked to Kong.

"Hi, Rosie. Hi, Brenda. How are you doing?" Flash asked.

"Hi, Flash," Brenda said. "Any clues?"

"No clues yet," he said.

Flash sat beside them on the curb.

"Hello, Kong," I said. "How are you doing, big guy?"

"Scratch, it's good to see you," Kong said. "I'm just fine, how about you?"

"Couldn't be better."

By the way, I wasn't talking to Kong like humans talk. No. We dogs talk silently. We use a kind of sign language. When I move my ears, eyes, nose, tongue, feet, and tail in certain ways it means something to other dogs. Get it? Well, it's complicated—except to us dogs. Anyway, that's how Kong and I talked to each other without Flash or Brenda or Rosie understanding anything we said. I mean, we could have been calling them all mudfaces and they wouldn't have known the difference. Arroo!

"So, Kong, have you seen Rosie's cats around?" I asked.

"Me? No way. Who'd want to actually go *looking* for cats? A dog's gotta be nuts to look for cats...oh, sorry, Scratch. I forgot that you're looking for cats. But you're on a case, right? So that's okay. Still, what a terrible thing to be looking for."

"I can handle it," I said.

Kong nodded knowingly.

Rosie said to Flash, "So what now, Flash? What will we do?"

"We've gotta stay calm," said Flash. "Flash Fry's on the case, so don't worry."

"Great," said Brenda. "Aren't you the same Flash Fry who had her cats in your hands but chucked them in the woods to start this whole mess?"

Flash's head fell and he nodded. "Yeah, that's me."

"Oh, Brenda, Flash didn't know they were mine," Rosie said. "It's not his fault."

Boy, Flash really felt bad about this whole thing. I sure did feel sorry for him. I gave him a few

30

cheek-licks and a nice nuzzle and he managed a smile.

"But I'm not giving up!" Flash suddenly said, scaring all of us.

Kong nudged me. "Your boy's a little weird around the edges, isn't he?"

"I guess," I said. "But I love him anyway."

Kong nodded. "We've got to expect that from humans."

"That's why I'm here," Flash said. "We've got to move into high gear on the case, and you two can help me!"

"How? How?" Rosie and Brenda said.

"Well, um..." Flash said. "I had a plan before I came over here, but now it seems to have slipped my mind. Gimme a second."

"Geesh!" huffed Brenda.

It's not that Flash is stupid or anything. Actually, he's pretty smart. It's just that every once in a while he forgets he's smart.

"Oh, yeah!" Flash blurted after a minute or two. "Rosie, do you have any photographs of Curly, Larry, and Moe?"

"Sure," she said, "Mom has lots. Why?"

"You'll see!" Flash said. "I'll follow you home and get the pictures. Then, I'm going to swing into action. If those cats are on the face of the earth, I'll find them."

"Flash, I'd come with you when you swing into action but I have to take Kong home and do some chores," Brenda said.

"Flash, can I go with you?" Rosie asked.

"Sure, why not. Four legs are better than two."

Don't I know it! I thought.

"Okay," Flash said, "let's move out!"

31

Flash and Rosie said good-bye to Brenda.

"Well, Scratch," Kong said, "I'll be sniffing you around."

"Listen, Kong, if you happen to see Rosie's cats, give me a howl, okay?"

"Will do, buddy. Take care of your hair. And don't bite any old bones!" Kong said, being dragged away by Brenda.

I laughed. "And don't you bark up any wrong trees!"

He laughed. We waved to each other with our tongues and went our separate ways. What a great dogfriend.

"What's your plan, Flash?" Rosie asked excitedly.

On our way to Rosie's house, Flash explained exactly what he wanted to do with the pictures of The Three Stooges and the rest of his plan.

"Perfect!" Rosie chirped, smiling for the first time that day.

Even I had to admit that it was the best plan Flash Fry had come up with in a long time.

Five: Tracking Cats

Flash and I both knew that Rosie's mother was hopping mad because her cats were missing, so we waited out on the sidewalk while Rosie went inside to search around for the pictures of the furry things. She came back out with dozens. Flash chose several photos, and Rosie took the rest back inside and returned to us.

"What first?" she asked.

"The newspaper," Flash said.

We walked to the local newspaper office, called *The News,* which was only about a half mile away, next to the laundromat and the huge grocery store. Flash adjusted his green hat and led us inside. I'd never seen a newspaper office, but this one looked small. Only three people were in the room directly in front of us. A woman was on the phone taking notes, a man was furiously typing at a word processor, and a fat, curly-haired man was walking toward us.

"May I help you kids?" he asked.

"Yes," said Rosie.

Flash glared at her and she stepped back. "Yes," said Flash. "My name is Flash Fry, Private Eye. This is Rosie McRoy, my client. It appears that her mother's three cats have vanished under mysterious circumstances, and we would like to place an ad, hoping that anyone who's seen them will call me."

The fat man chuckled. "I see. A very serious matter, indeed. Indeed. What kind of ad would you like to place?"

"A lost kitty ad," Flash replied.

"No, no. I mean, what size. How many lines? One column or two?"

Flash paused. "I'll have to consult with my client." Flash whispered to Rosie, and she whispered to him. Flash addressed the fat man again. "We don't know what you're talking about."

"Okay," said the fat man, smiling. "Tell me what you want and I'll help you with it."

Flash handed the man photos of The Three Stooges. "Here are photos of the missing cats. Their descriptions are on the backs. I guess we should keep it simple. Something like: LOST CATS. IF YOU'VE SEEN THEM, CALL FLASH FRY, PRIVATE EYE."

"Good idea," said the fat man. "Keep it short and to the point. Maybe nice big type beside a group photograph. Two columns, I'd say, ought to do it. And you'll want to add your phone number."

"Right," said Flash. The fat man handed Flash a pen and he wrote his number on the back of one photo. "Is that all?"

"Everything but payment," said the fat man. "Let's see now. Hmmm. You can run it for one week, which is the minimum. If the cats aren't found in a week, then you can run it again. Sound good?"

"Yes," Flash said. "Will it run today?"

"Oh, no! What's this, Saturday? Earliest I can get it in is Monday."

"There goes the big game," said Rosie.

"Well, we might not find them in time anyway, Rosie," said Flash. "I think we should still run the ad."

"Okay."

"Okay," Flash said to the fat man. "How much will that be?"

The fat man did some figuring in the air with his finger. "Ten dollars and sixty cents."

"WHAT!" Flash said. "I don't have that much."

"Me, either," Rosie said. Tears erupted in her eyes. "I'll never find my cats. And Mom will kill me if they don't turn up. I just don't know what I'm going to do if—"

"Easy, easy," said the fat man. He rubbed his chubby face as he thought. His eyes lit up. "I've got it! I'll write a story. A news item, picture and all. FAITHFUL CATS MYSTERIOUSLY VANISH. NO CLUES. OWNERS ASK THE PUBLIC FOR HELP. Something like that."

"That's great!" Flash said. "How much would that cost?"

"Why, nothing," the fat man said. "It's news. We print the news for nothing. All you have to do is buy a paper on Monday. And even though the story will run only once, many more people will notice it."

Flash held out his hand and the fat man shook it. "Thank you very much," Flash said. He turned to us. "Let's go, gang. Lots to do! Bye."

"So long, Mr. Fry," said the fat man, waving his hand and jiggling all over.

Back outside, the clouds overhead seemed to have gotten thicker. My knees tingled, my tail felt heavy, and my nose was wet. Yup, it was going to rain all right. I sniffed around the entrance of *The News* a little, found half a lollypop in the bushes, and ate it.

"All set for the next step?" Flash asked.

"Yup!" Rosie said.

"Okay. You take one photo and I'll take another. You hit the grocery store and I'll get the laundromat. Both are packed with people, and we might just get lucky. Ready? Let's move out!"

"Good luck!" Rosie shouted over her shoulder as she sprinted for the grocery store doors.

"Now, Scratch, let's swing into action."

The laundromat was packed and noisy. The washers were *shug-shug-shug*ging. The dryers were *kadumm-kadumm-kadumm*ing. A radio was blasting. And people all over the laundromat were talking in loud voices over the many other noises.

Flash approached an older woman sitting on a bench reading a magazine and eating a candy bar. "Excuse me, ma'am, but—"

"WHAT?"

"Excuse me, but—"

"WHAT? CAN'T HEAR YOU!" And she pointed at the washer next to her head.

"I said, excuse me, but—"

"SPEAK UP, BOY!"

Flash shoved the picture of the cats in front of

her face. Then he leaned over close to her ear and shouted, "LOST CATS!"

"YOU DON'T HAVE TO SCREAM, SON. NO, I HAVEN'T LOST THESE CATS."

"I MEAN," screamed Flash, "HAVE YOU SEEN THEM? MY FRIEND LOST THEM."

She shook her head no and went back to reading her magazine.

Flash next approached two men talking over by the quieter dryers.

"Excuse me," Flash said.

"Great hat," said one man.

"Thanks," said Flash. "I'm Flash Fry, Private Eye. This is my dog, Scratch, Private Nose."

"Pleased to meet you," said the other man. "What can we do for you?"

Flash held out the photo. "My client has lost these cats and really needs to find them. Have you seen them around town?"

The men studied the picture and said at the same time: "No."

Person by person, Flash made his way around the laundromat, and when he was done no one had seen Rosie's cats. He wandered sadly outside and sat on a bench next to a phone booth. "Maybe Rosie had better luck," he said.

"Washing your undies, Flash?"

I knew that voice and wished I hadn't heard it. It belonged to Brick Glick.

"What are you doing here, Brick?" Flash asked.

"I was just buying some health food in the grocery store," he said. "Us baseball stars have to keep healthy, you know. I saw Rosie in there showing a picture of her cats around, so I figured you weren't far away. I was right."

38

"Lucky me," Flash said.

"Flash, you're used to being embarrassed, but I'm not," Brick said. "I kind of hope Rosie doesn't find her cats so we don't have to play the game and be smeared by the Tornadoes."

"You know, Brick," said Flash, "you're not too bad a baseball player, even if you're not great. But you're good enough to know that anything can happen in a baseball game, especially if the whole team is trying. I think we might win the game."

"Ha! We've lost all our games. What makes you think we can beat the first-place, undefeated team?"

"Because," Flash said, "we have to. Because we want to so much we can taste it. And because they think we'll be easy to beat. We'd have a lot better chance if you'd have more team spirit."

"Impossible," said Brick. "I'm tired of being embarrassed all the time by losing."

"Brick, you're starting to repeat yourself," Flash said. "By the way, how's your hand?"

Brick flexed his fingers. "Okay. But if you're going to pitch, Flash, I hope the other team has an ambulance there! Have fun chasing cats." And Brick walked away laughing.

I sensed that Flash was going to yell something really dumb at Brick, and I was prepared to run after him and jump on him or something, when Rosie came up looking sad.

"No luck," she said, hanging her redheaded head. "Nothing at all. Not even close."

"Well, take it from me, kid," Flash said. "Nobody said this private eye work was easy. Let's stick with it. Let's head for my house. We'll stop in every house along the way and show them the pictures.

39

I've already asked all of them, but maybe the pictures will ring a bell. Then we'll stop by the stationery store on the corner and put the next phase of my plan into action. Okay?"

"Okay," Rosie said.

A half hour later we were working on the dining room table at Flash's house. No one we showed any of the pictures to had seen the cats. Now, Flash and Rosie were making posters. At the stationery store, Flash had made twenty photocopies of the cat photos, and they looked pretty good, too. Then Rosie bought some poster board and marking pens. Now they were pasting the photos on the poster board and making signs for the lost cats. The posters read:

LOST: 3 CATS

1. ORANGE WITH YELLOW STRIPES LIKE A TIGER
2. BLACK WITH WHITE AROUND A
    SMALL BLACK NOSE
3. KIND OF MIXED-UP BROWN WITH
    BLACK FEET LIKE SHOES

THEIR NAMES ARE CURLY, LARRY, AND MOE.
IF SEEN OR FOUND, PLEASE CALL THE NUMBER BELOW

Flash and Rosie argued about whose phone number should go on the posters, and they agreed that Rosie would probably be home more than Flash, and if Rosie wasn't then her mother would be. They put Rosie's number on the poster. They also agreed that they should have given *The News* Rosie's number too, so Flash called and gave the fat man her number for the story.

When the posters were done, they split up and hung them all over town. Then they met back at Flash's house.

"Hope we get a phone call soon," Flash said.

"Well, I'd better be home to get it! Bye!" said Rosie.

After Rosie left, Flash paced and paced around his front lawn. I didn't pace with him. I found a nice cool place under the shrubbery and snuggled in.

"I'm forgetting something, Scratch, I know I am," he said.

I knew he was, too. It was probably the first thing he should have done. Naturally, I had it figured out a long time ago, but I couldn't say anything to him, could I? So, as usual, I just had to wait for Flash to figure it out on his own. He usually does, but it takes a bit of time.

"Let's backtrack a little," Flash said. "Now. Rosie's cats are gone. That means that they are either lost or stolen or . . . or what? Or . . . Or someone found them! Yeah! Now, what would someone do if they found three cats? Well, if it was me, I'd throw them in the woods like a jerk. No, somebody else might . . . might what? What do you do with lost cats you found? Why, you take them to the Lost and Found! No . . . there's a name for that kind of place. Hmmmm. Oh, yeah: the pound! They'd take them to the city pound. I've got to go check out the city pound. Maybe that's why the cats never came back —because someone took them to the city pound. What a brain! What a private eye! Let's go, Scratch. Flash Fry is on the case again!"

See, like I said. It takes a bit of time.

Me, I thought the cats were at the pound—actually, in this town they call it a shelter. Why did I think that? Mainly because we didn't have any other clues. No suspects. No nothing. Yeah, I would have bet my tail that the cats were at the pound.

Good thing I didn't bet. I would have looked really silly.

"Lunchtime!" Flash's mother hollered.

My second-favorite word in the world. My first favorite word is "Dinnertime!"

So, we ate.

Six: Cats in Cages

Lunch was over and I felt lazy and full. But Flash was on a case, and I had to help him or he'd be lost.

Flash and I stepped into his garage. "It's 1:27," Flash said. "Less than twenty-four hours until the big game. Take away about ten hours for sleeping tonight, and tomorrow morning is shot with breakfast and Sunday school and lunch, so that really leaves about, ummmmm, eight or nine hours! Gotta hurry."

Flash walked over to his bike. "Gotta fix this flat tire. It'll save time if we ride."

Twenty minutes later, we were rolling. He'd lifted me up into the basket on the handlebars, and we were zooming along to the city pound. If I had long ears, they'd have been flapping in Flash's face.

Flash rode hard, and after about a mile and half he coasted up a long driveway off the main road.

43

The sign out front said CITY ANIMAL SHELTER. The building was brick and one story tall. Already I could hear dogs barking and cats meowing and a few hamsters hamming, or whatever they do.

Flash and I went through the front door and found ourselves in a large waiting room with a concrete floor with a drain in the middle. Inside, the barking and meowing sounds were ten times as loud. The place smelled like animals—their fur, their food, and various other scents that people find disgusting but animals are used to.

Flash sneezed loudly. *"AH-CHOO! CHOO!* Darn. This case is a real pain for someone who's allergic to cats."

He walked up to a window in the wall, behind which stood a young woman reading a paperback book.

"Excuse me," he said.

She peered over her book at Flash, then she looked down at me, then back to Flash. "I hope you're not here to give up your cute dog."

"No!" Flash said. "I'd never give him up!"

Awwww. That's why I love him.

"No, I'm here to find some animals who are lost. Some cats. Three cats, to be exact."

"What do they look like?" she asked.

"Well, one is orange with yellow stripes, one is black with a white nose, and one is brown with black feet. Their names are Curly, Larry, and Moe."

The young woman laughed. "Doesn't matter with cats what their names are, don't you know that? You could call them mud, spit, and drool, and it wouldn't matter to cats. They have their own real names among themselves and that's all that matters."

44

I was surprised. She was right! Dogs have their own names among themselves, too. My name is *Arf-grrrr-yip* with a left-side tongue-hang. Would a human ever think to name his dog *Arf-grrrr-yip* with a left-side tongue-hang? I doubt it.

"Are the cats here?" Flash asked. "Have you seen them?"

"They come, they go," said the woman. "I can't afford to notice too many of them. I get to like them and then...well, and then if no one comes... well..."

"Well, what?" Flash asked.

"Well, I hate to see an animal I like put to sleep."

"To sleep?" Flash asked.

"Killed," said the young woman. "A fatal injection. There's nothing else we can do with homeless animals who aren't claimed. It's such a shame, especially when the animals are free to whoever wants them."

I'd never known they did that to lost animals. I immediately licked Flash's hand and rubbed up against his leg. I loved him, and was sure glad I had a good home.

"Killed..." Flash said, thinking over what she'd said, too.

"Want to look for your cats?" asked the young woman.

"AH-CHOO! Sure. Can my dog come?"

"Well," she said, "since the boss isn't here, sure he can come. If he behaves himself. If not, he has to wait outside. But we have to be quick, okay?"

"That's okay with—*AH-CHOO!*—me," Flash said.

The young woman disappeared from the window

45

and the door opened beside it. She was there, waving us forward.

"Be good, Scratch," Flash said. He whipped out one of his father's handkerchiefs that he'd snatched at home earlier and blew his nose.

We followed the woman down a long hallway. The animal noises were booming all over the place.

"They're noisy because they're hungry," the young woman yelled. "It's feeding time!"

"AH-AH-CHOOOOOO!" Flash replied.

Besides the things I mentioned before, I smelled other things. Like fear. And worry. And loneliness. But that wasn't the worst thing. I'll tell you right now, it is a good thing humans don't understand animal talk, because it would tear your heart out in a place like this. I heard dogs begging to be let out, asking why they were locked up, why they weren't being fed. I heard puppies and kittens screaming for their mothers. Grown cats were crying, and old dogs were trying to cheer them up. I already hated being there, but I had to stick with Flash. I felt like the luckiest dog in the world because I wasn't in one of those horrible cages. But still, I knew all these cats and dogs would face more horrible things if they were still on the loose and starving.

"AH-CHOO!"

"Bless you," said the woman to Flash, who'd just sneezed off his green hat. She pointed to the right, down the hall that led between the long row of cages of animals. "If your cats are here, they'd be in one of those cages. Go on down and see if they're here, but please make it fast, okay?"

"Thank *CHOO!*"

She giggled. "You're welcome."

I stuck close by Flash's leg, trying not to hear the

46

pleading voices yelling down at me from the cages. Wide-eyed faces peered out at us and ears perked up. Every type of dog was there. Huge, little, young, old, angry, sad, nice, mean. Cats too, in all colors and sizes, were stuffed into the cages, which, actually, were pretty clean. From some cages the smells of medicine wafted out. At least a doctor was taking care of the sick guys. As we passed by, I said "Hiya" or "Hang in there."

Poor Flash was sneezing like crazy, like a train, nonstop. But he took the time to peer into every cage for The Three Stooges. Sometimes he would *Ah* and *Ooo* at the cute animals, then move on. Before I knew it, we had turned around and were almost at the end.

Flash said, "Not here." He blew his nose hard, then made frog noises in his throat.

"Sorry," said the young woman. "Thanks for coming. See anything else you might like to give a home?"

"Yeah," Flash said with a sniffly nose. "All of them."

Soon we were back out in the gray day. Flash was taking deep breaths of the fresh air, and I was trying to figure out how long until it started raining.

"Hi, Flash!" someone said to our right.

Me, I'd smelled him a few moments ago. It was Pete Hurthwurst, one of Flash's best buddies, the practical joker. He was standing beside his shiny bike.

"Hi, Pete," Flash said. "What are you doing out here?"

"I don't know," Pete said. "I got bored so I just took a ride."

"Bored?" Flash said.

47

Pete's family is probably the richest family in town. A mansion. Servants. The works. Pete's bedroom looks like an arcade and a playroom rolled into one. He gets anything in the world he wants. And now he was bored. Some kids never have enough! Me, give me a bone and an old blanket to curl up on and that's all I need. Well, a radio wouldn't hurt either.

"What are you doing at the pound, Flash?"

"Looking for Rosie's cats. They're not there. I'm at another dead end. How the heck does anyone find cats?"

Pete thought about that. "Beats me. If I find out, though, I'll let you know."

"So what do I do now?" Flash asked.

"Beats me," Pete said again. "You're the detective. Oh, well, you're no fun, so I guess I'll keep rolling. By the way, I've seen a lot of Lasers looking for the cats, too. Maybe I'll go check around myself. Hey, too bad you can't just kind of lure the cats back to your house, huh? Wouldn't it be great to have a second chance at catching them? Oh, well. Good luck!"

"Thanks, Pete."

And Pete rolled off on his glittering, expensive bike.

"Hmmmmmm," Flash said.

There was an idea simmering in Flash's mind and I knew what it was. There was a slim possibility that we could get Rosie's cats back into our house, but Flash had to put two and two together. I tried to help.

I barked three times and leapt around in a small circle.

Flash frowned. "Scratch, this is no time to beg for

food. Can't you see I'm thinking about the cats?"

I barked three more times in a circle.

"What the heck is the matter with you?" Flash asked angrily. "Boy, Scratch, sometimes you really are a pain. Cats don't jump around like that for their food..."

He was almost there. He almost had the idea. I waited.

"Hold on now," Flash said, pacing around, taking his hat off, putting it on, taking it off, putting it on again. "If...yes, if the cats came for food the first time, why not again? Maybe I can get them back to the house again with food! And then catch them!"

He grabbed me around the belly and lifted me up into the bike basket. "Let's go, Scratch! Flash Fry, Private Eye, has another brilliant idea!"

But we all really know who had the idea. Right, gang? Woof!

Seven: Cats Come, Cats Go, Cats Come

When we got home, Flash jumped off his bike and hustled toward the front door. Just as he got to it, it opened. Flash's tall, thin father stood there with sawdust in his hair, bandages on his fingers, and a smile on his face. "Picnic table's done!" he announced. "Come on down and see it."

Flash beamed. "Does this mean I get my office back?"

"I guess so. I've swept up all the sawdust and stuff. But you have to promise to stay away from the table. It's drying."

"Oh, boy!"

We went downstairs in the basement to look at the picnic table Flash's father built. It looked like a picnic table. It was all shiny and wet with a fresh coat of wood stain. I hate wood stain. It stinks. It stinks to the moon. It clogs up my nose and makes

51

my eyes water. It stinks, and it stank right then. I sneezed. I snorted. I yawned. Nothing was unclogging my nose. Dogs are nothing without their noses, especially detective dogs like me. I had to think of something fast, like running away. Then Flash's father went to the basement window and opened it wide. I could have licked his face a thousand times. Fresh air came wafting down into my sniffing nose. Ahhh.

"It's the best picnic table I ever saw," said Flash.

His father smiled, looking at his work, "Yeah, it is, isn't it. Just be careful of the wet stain, okay? See you later." He went upstairs.

Flash settled back onto his onion crate chair and put his feet up on his card table desk. "Sure is good to have my old office back!" He cranked down the handle of the old Coke machine to his left and down thudded a grape soda. He twisted off the cap and took a long sip, then smacked his lips just to torture me. Do I get grape soda? No way.

Flash picked up the phone on his desk and dialed. "Hello, Rosie? Any luck on your end? You saw a wedding coming out of a church and you ran up and showed them the pictures of The Three Stooges? And they got mad? Gee, I wonder why. No, I didn't have any luck either. But I do have a good idea. Keep your fingers crossed. Bye!"

Flash wasted no time putting his plan to lure Rosie's cats to our house into action. First, he went upstairs, snuck into the kitchen, and got four small bowls. Next, from the cabinets he took three cans of tuna fish, carefully opened them on the electric can opener, then rushed back downstairs. He scooped half a can of tuna into each bowl and set the bowls on a tabletop about two feet below the basement

52

window. He still had one can of tuna left.

"It's perfect!" Flash said. "Next, I'll take this last can of tuna and drop a trail of tuna from the window to the woods, another trail to the east, and another trail to the west. If the cats are out there, they'll smell the trail of tuna, follow it to the basement window, smell the bowls of tuna, hop down into the basement, and I've got them! Flash Fry strikes again!"

Me, I laughed to myself. There were a few things wrong with his plan, but I couldn't say anything. All I could do was hope they didn't happen.

So, I followed Flash around outside and he dropped his trail of tuna fish. I also lifted my leg against a few favorite bushes and dug inside a gopher hole until Flash yelled at me to stop. Then we went back inside the basement to wait.

"We have to be very quiet," Flash said to me. He sat at his desk and put his feet up. "Half of being a detective is knowing how to wait. Remember that."

Yeah, I sure would.

"This plan, Scratch," Flash whispered, "is what you call a calculated gamble. We run the risk of luring other animals to our house, but the way I figure it is that if Rosie's cats are lost out there, they are hungry. They are probably, by now, hungrier than any other animal out there. So, they will most likely be the animals to come first. Not bad, huh?"

See, Flash doesn't understand animals very well. He doesn't understand that *all* animals are hungry almost *all* the time. Any second now, fifteen squirrels might come scampering through the window. Or a skunk. Heck, *I* was having a hard time not bounding up to the window and gobbling down the tuna. But I didn't. I was curious to see what ended up coming through that window.

So, we waited.

Flash and I must have dozed off, because when I woke up I heard lapping sounds. The sounds of animals licking food. Tuna food. I took a look.

"Cats!" Flash yelped. "*AH-CHOO!* Oh, no! Oh, no!" He hopped up and did a little confused dance by his desk, sneezing.

There were about fifteen cats in the basement. They were lapping at the bowls of tuna fish, exploring boxes and shelves, and sniffing around on top of the sticky picnic table.

"Oh, no!" Flash went on, trying to whisper his screams. "The-the—*AH-CHOO!*—table! It's full of hair and covered with pawprints! Oh, no! And what's that at the window?"

Outside the window, a huge brown dog was licking the tuna off the grass and trying to shove its immense head into the small window. It was snuffling like crazy, its long tongue lolling inside trying to reach down to the bowls.

I barked once, showed my teeth, let one ear fall, and stood up. What I said was: "Beat it, fang-face."

The big dog looked down at me, shrugged, smiled, and loped away. Meanwhile, the mob of cats had taken over the basement.

Flash was holding his head, sneezing, and muttering to himself. "What have I done? What a dumb idea! Why did I ever lure cats down here with Dad's sticky table? Worse, none of them are Rosie's cats! Oh, why didn't I *think?* Dad will kill me! He might even punish me! *AH-CHOO!* Gotta think of something fast!"

The first thing he did was open the basement

doors and try to shoo the cats out. A few left, but most of them paid no attention. Then he grabbed one, put it outside, came back for the other one, put it outside while watching the first one run back inside, and so on. The cats refused to leave the basement.

He blew his nose hard and said, "Think!"

While Flash had his eyes squeezed tight in thought, I grabbed one of the bowls of tuna fish, got the cats' attention, and ran outside with it. Most of the cats followed me out.

Flash opened his eyes and smiled. "Hey, good thinking, Scratch!"

Now there were two cats left. One was all white with a black tip on its tail and a ragged ear. The other was really skinny and gray, with a white belly.

I moved over to one cat and tried to talk cat-talk. It laughed at me. Then I growled and it began to back up into a corner. I went over to the other cat and growled until I had both cats backed into a corner. Flash took the cue, picked up the cats, and dumped them into a cardboard box. He closed the lid. Plenty of air could get in, but the cats weren't going anywhere.

"Good work, Scratch!" Flash said. *"CHOO!* Now, the table."

Flash closed the back door, took away the tuna bowls, then started to pick the cat hairs off the sticky picnic table with a pair of small pliers he found on his father's workbench. After he'd picked off the hairs, he opened a can of wood stain and brushed a thin coat on the tabletop.

"Perfect! Now, the cats." Flash grabbed the box of cats and carried it up the basement steps and outside. "I just don't have the heart to dump them in the woods, especially after what the lady at the shelter told us. *AH-CHOO!*" He thought some more. "If I only knew who the owners were I could return the cats."

I could have bitten myself. Why didn't I think of that? Me, with the super-sniffing nose. Sure, I could sniff the trail of the cats backward to their homes! It was the only choice we had. Scratch to the rescue.

I started sniffing the grass. Immediately, I picked up the scents of the two cats we had. There was only one problem. Flash wasn't following me. He was still standing there, thinking.

Well, like all smart dogs, I've got my master trained. If I bark three times and dance in a circle, he knows I'm hungry. If I bark by the back door, he knows I have to go out. And if I bark and run away, he always follows.

I barked five times, put my nose to the ground, then started trotting away.

"Hey, Scratch, what's up? Smell something? Hey, wait up!"

Flash, with the box of cats, started running after me. He didn't really know why he was following me, or where he was going, but, like I said, I've got him trained.

We wound our way in and out of the woods, under bushes, through a sandbox, over a car, around many trees.

"I get it!" Flash said about fifteen minutes later. "You're sniffing out the cats' trail! Maybe it will lead us to their homes. Good boy, Scratch!"

What would he do without me?

Soon the trail ended at a red front door. After all that tracking, we were only about eight houses down from Flash's house. Flash knocked on the door. It opened.

"Well, now, aren't you Flash Fry from down the street?" said a smiling old woman with short gray hair. "Sure you are. I know your parents. Very nice people, they are. Do you remember me? I guess not. I'm Mrs. Wain. Are you selling something?"

"*AH-CHOO!*" Flash said.

"Bless you, poor boy."

"Thanks," Flash said. "No, I'm not selling anything. See, I was out looking for Rosie McRoy's three cats and—"

"Oh, yes. I've seen the posters all over town. Haven't found them yet? Too bad. Strange, though, just a few moments ago I looked for my two kitties and couldn't find them either."

"Uh, I think they're in this box," Flash said.

"Really!" said Mrs. Wain.

What luck, I thought. Both cats belong to the same person.

"Oh, they *are* mine! What are *you* doing with them? Eh? Speak up, young man."

"Well, um, it's kind of hard to explain," Flash said. "They were around my house, um, and—"

"Oh, one can never believe the tales you kids tell anyway. Give them here. Well, I guess I should thank you properly. Wait there a second." Mrs. Wain dropped her cats inside and closed the door. We waited there for a couple of minutes and then she reappeared. "Here, this is for finding my cats," she said. She held out three dollar bills to Flash.

"Hey, I couldn't take that," Flash said, blushing. "I didn't do anything."

"You took the trouble to return my cats," she said. "And with all the nasty kids in the world, I

58

think I should encourage all the children I can to do good deeds. Take it!"

Flash took the money. "Thank you very much!"

Mrs. Wain said good-bye and we started walking back home. Coming toward us along the sidewalk were Curtis and Gene, two of Flash's teammates.

"Flash!" Gene said. "We were just over at your house."

"Yeah," said Curtis. "Find Rosie's cats yet?"

"Not yet," Flash said.

"You know we're running out of time fast," said Curtis.

"I know, I know, I know," Flash said.

"So why aren't you looking?" asked Gene. "Why are you wandering around the sidewalk with your dumb dog?"

I growled.

"I mean, your nice doggie?"

"I just came from Mrs. Wain's," Flash said. "I found her cats and gave them back to her.

"What!" Curtis said. "You're supposed to be finding *Rosie's* cats, not Mrs. Wain's! Why are you wasting time finding the wrong cats?"

"I—"

"Some detective," Gene said. "Well, we're going over to the city pound to see if the cats are there. If you were a good detective, you would have thought of that, too! Let's go, Curtis."

"But . . ." Flash said.

And Gene and Curtis stormed off. They'd soon feel like jerks when they found out Flash had been there ahead of them.

Flash and I continued on home. Once there, he closed the back basement doors and gave the table one more check. Just as he sat back down at his desk, something came through the basement window.

A cat. Then another cat plopped down.

"Mrs. Wain's cats are back!" Flash said.

This time, he didn't waste a second. He sprinted to the cats, grabbed them by the scruff of their necks, put one under each arm, kicked open the basement doors and hustled all the way back to Mrs. Wain's house, sneezing like crazy. He rang Mrs. Wain's doorbell with his nose.

"Oh, my!" Mrs Wain said when she saw Flash with her cats.

"I guess you shouldn't have let them out so soon," Flash said. "They must have followed me back. Better keep them inside for a while."

She eyes Flash suspiciously. "I'm not giving you another reward, young man."

"I don't want one!" he said. "I'm just returning your cats again, that's—*AH-CHOO!*—all. Sorry. Bye."

This time, when we got back home Flash closed the basement window. The smell of the wood stain was too much for us so we went upstairs into the living room. It was almost four-thirty.

"We've only got four, maybe five, hours left to find the cats and get Rosie back in the game," said Flash. "But what am I gonna do now?"

Flash's dad wasn't around, so I hopped up into his favorite chair. Flash slumped down into the sofa. He took off his detective hat and scratched his head. He was frowning. He was also out of ideas. I felt sorry for him.

I left the chair and slid up beside him on the couch and put my head in his lap. He began to pet me behind both ears. Ahhh! More! More! I rolled over so I was looking up at him with my big sad eyes. He began to rub and scratch my tummy. Ooooo! Ahhhh! My back left leg started running on its own. Ooooo, that tickles!

Suddenly Flash stopped. He lifted me off his lap and stood, leaving me sprawled belly-up on the sofa. He walked to the phone, lifted the receiver, and pushed the buttons hard.

"Hello. Is Pete there? Thanks. Pete? It's Flash. I'm calling an emergency meeting. We have to call the team. Everyone has to be there. Yes, even Brick. I'll call the girls, you call the guys. Tell them to be at your place in fifteen minutes. Yes, you bet this is serious! See ya."

Flash hung up and just stood there a minute. Then he looked over at me. I was still on my back, legs spread, looking at him upside-down with my tongue hanging out. I wagged my stubby tail.

"Scratch, you look ridiculous."

He jumped me, we wrestled on the floor for a few minutes, then he called the girls.

Eight: The Tree Mansion

Like I said, Pete Hurthwurst is rich. I mean, very rich. I mean, his house looks like the White House. Flash and I pulled up the long driveway on his bike. He lifted me out of the basket, then dropped his bike on the perfect green lawn. The sky was grayer. It was filling up with rain.

While Flash walked up to the huge front door, I chased a butterfly around the front yard until it turned and started chasing me.

The front door opened and one of my favorite humans stood in the doorway. He was Rowland, the Hurthwurst family butler. I ran up to the door to greet him.

"Ah, Master Flash and Scratch. Good to see you," said Rowland. He bent down and rubbed the sides of my face, I licked his chin, and he laughed and rubbed me some more. Then he stood and straightened his uniform. "I presume you are looking for Master Peter?"

"Yes," Flash said.

Rowland pointed a thumb toward the back of the house. "He's around back, and up."

"You mean, he's in the attic?" Flash asked.

Rowland smiled patiently. "No, he's in his tree-house."

"Oh! Yeah, sure, of course," Flash said. "Thank you, Rowland."

"It was nothing," he said. He gave me one last pat, then closed the front door.

Flash and I followed a narrow flagstone sidewalk down the long side of the mansion and through a hedge, where we emerged into the backyard, which was about the size of a baseball field with lots of towering trees and blooming flowers.

There, twenty feet up in the tallest, strongest tree, was Pete's magnificent treehouse. It was a mansion treehouse. It had lots of windows, a shingled roof, white outside walls, and a red front door.

Pete's face, framed with his fiery red hair, suddenly appeared in one of the windows. "Hi, Flash! You're late! Come on up!"

I knew we weren't late. What he meant was that everyone else was already up there. Anytime any of us has a chance to visit Pete's treehouse, we come over as fast as we can.

A trapdoor in the bottom of the tree mansion opened and a seat like you find on a ferris wheel was lowered down on chains by a motor I heard whirring above. The seat stopped about three feet from the ground. We got in and lowered the safety bar in front of us. With a slight jerk, the seat began to rise. I should have been scared, because dogs

64

aren't used to heights, but I wasn't. I'm tough. I also had my eyes closed.

"This is great," Flash said. "It must be terrific to be rich."

Yeah, I thought. So why was Pete so bored earlier?

The seat lifted us up right through the floor of the tree mansion and inside. The trapdoor closed and bolted below us. We raised the safety bar and stepped out.

"Welcome to Pete's Treetop Hideaway," Pete said. "There's soda and chips in the other room, and ice water and doggie treats for the mutt."

For doggie treats, I'll let him call me a mutt once.

I took a few sniffs. It all smelled clean and freshly polished and a little bit like Rowland. I guess he rode the seat up to clean up here. He was probably the only one of the house staff brave enough. What a guy. We stood in a small room, and in front of us was a larger L-shaped room with comfortable chairs, a TV set, plenty of video games, and lots of other stuff for human kids to play with. Against the far wall under one of the windows was a desk covered with rubber worms, hand buzzers, snapping gum, smoke bombs, fake dog poop and throw-up, and a bunch of other practical jokes Pete loved to play on people. Rock music played in the background from hidden speakers.

All of Flash's teammates were in the other room. Even quiet George. That was a surprise, because we never see him except at ball games, but I guess that's what quiet kids are all about. He's a good catcher, though.

"About time you got here," said Curtis.

"I figured you'd be here early if there was food,

65

Curtis," Flash said. Everyone chuckled, and Curtis stuffed some pretzels in his cheeks.

Flash approached an empty chair, but before he sat he smiled and lifted the cushion and peered underneath. "What? No whoopie cushion? No gags?"

"You said this was a serious meeting," Pete said. "Here, have some soda."

"Thanks," said Flash, taking the glass. "I'm proud of you, Pete. It *is* a serious meeting. Very serious." Flash lifted the glass to take a sip and soda spilled all over the front of his shirt. "Hey! A dribble glass! I should have known."

Pete was rolling around on the floor laughing, and so was everyone else. Pete tossed Flash a towel and said, *"Now* it's a serious meeting."

Me, I was gobbling down doggie treats as fast as I could. Pete had the best doggie treats in the world. Yum-yum. When I'd finished them, I curled up in a corner to listen.

"So, why are we all here?" asked Marybeth, Pete's snotty sister.

"I wouldn't have come, but I had nothing better to do," Brick said. "Besides, there's free food."

"Gee, Brick," Pete said, "you sure are a fun guy."

"Can it," said Curtis. "Let's get on with it."

"Time is running out," Rosie said.

"So, what's the word on Rosie's cats?" asked Gene.

"I was going to ask you all the same question," said Flash. "I called us here to get ideas, put our heads together. Anyone have any leads?"

"Not me." "Nope." "Nothing." "None," they said.

"Me, either," said Flash. "Scratch and Rosie and I looked all over the place, but nothing. It's weird."

"It sure is," Brick said.

66

"Yeah, but wanting to play in the big game isn't weird," Curtis said. "And if we don't find those cats, we'll have to forfeit the game 'cause we won't have nine players."

"It's better than losing," Brick said. "I don't know about you guys, but I'm not a loser."

"Brick," Flash said, "we haven't even played the game yet, so shut up, will you?"

"If we can get Rosie back on the team we have a chance," said Brenda. "But where the heck are Rosie's cats? I mean, this neighborhood isn't that large. We've asked everybody we've seen and no one has seen the cats at all. It's like they just vanished."

Gene said, "For all three to disappear completely at the same time, well, it's, well . . . "

"Weird," said Brenda.

"Any theories?" Flash asked.

"Yeah," Brick said. "People from outer space took them for experiments. They took the cats because they were the most intelligent life form they could find."

"Doesn't say much for you, Brick," said Curtis.

"Very funny," Brick growled.

"We're getting nowhere," said Marybeth.

"Well, even if we don't find my cats," said Rosie, "I wanna thank all you guys for looking so hard for them. I think we've got the best team in the world. Even you, Brick. You talk big, but you're here and you're a good ball player. Thanks."

All the kids blushed and mumbled. They didn't like mushy talk.

"We need ideas!" Flash blurted.

"There has to be something we're doing wrong," Pete said. "Something we've overlooked."

"But what?" asked Marybeth. "You either look

67

for cats, or you don't. You either find them, or you don't. They're either here, or they're not. What else can we do?"

"If we knew that, we'd do it, dummy," Pete said.

"Just because you're my know-it-all brother—" Marybeth began.

"No fights!" Flash said. "Come on, guys, think!"

"I have an idea," said quiet George.

"You do?" said the whole team.

He winced. "Yes. There's only one person who can help us. Flash has to go talk with...the cat woman."

Everyone said, "Oooooo, the cat woman!"

"You're crazy," Flash said.

"No," said Pete. "The cat woman is crazy. Living out there in the woods all alone. People say she's got a couple hundred cats out there."

"I've heard she *eats* them," Brick said.

"Weird," said Brenda.

"Forget it," said Flash. "Why should I go see that nutty woman?"

"I know why, and I think George has a great idea here," said Rosie. "Because she knows cats. My mother and I met her in the kitty litter section of the grocery store the other day. She didn't seem crazy to me. And she sure did know her kitty litter. We even bought the brand she recommended and it is much better than the brand we used to use."

"Oh boy, wonderful," said Brick.

"I agree with George and Rosie," Marybeth said. "As long as I don't have to go, too."

"I said forget it, and I meant it," Flash said. "No way."

"Gee," said Curtis, "you know, the cat woman might even have Rosie's cats."

"Hey, she might!" Gene said.

"Makes sense, you have to admit," said Mary-beth.

"Sure does," said George. "We can't find the cats anywhere else. The cat woman collects stray cats, so they really might be there. Flash, you have to go."

It seemed to me that there was no way out for poor Flash. He was the detective, and there were a couple of good reasons for him to take his investigation to the cat woman. Flash knew it, too.

"Oh, shoot, I guess you're right," Flash said. "Maybe the cat woman can give us some help. Maybe she did find the cats."

"Yeah," Brick said, "so you'd better get out there right away before she eats them!"

"Thanks, Brick," Flash said. "Okay, I'll go on one condition. Rosie, you have to come with me. You can talk to her a lot easier than I can. Besides, they're your cats."

"All right, I'll go," Rosie said.

"So, it's settled," Curtis said. "Let's eat!"

At 5:05, we all left Pete's tree mansion. Everyone wished Flash and Rosie good luck.

"I have to be home for dinner at six," Rosie said.

"Me, too," Flash said. "So, I guess we'd better get going, huh?"

Rosie gulped. "Yeah, I guess so."

Flash loaded me up in the basket on his bike, Rosie hopped on her bike, and we headed off to the outskirts of town and the cat woman's strange house, a house no other kid or dog had ever seen before.

A roll of thunder shook the dark gray sky.

Nine: The Cat Woman

I love riding in the basket on the front of Flash's bike, did I ever tell you that? Well, I do. All sorts of exciting things fly into my face—some of which I eat—but the very best thing is the breeze. I love how the wind of Flash's speed pushes my ears back and combs through my fur and fills my nostrils and mouth. And if I hang my tongue out, I'm instantly cooled off by the breeze on my tongue. It's great. Flash likes it when I ride up front, too, because I stop all the bugs from hitting his face.

Flash was riding beside Rosie, and as we whizzed down a hill and picked up speed, I hung out my tongue and began panting. Flash and Rosie decided it was a good time to talk.

"Is your mom really mad?" Flash said loudly over the rush of wind, while holding on to his green detective hat with one hand.

"Really," Rosie said. "She's mad at me because I let the cats get out. If we don't find them...I don't want to think about that."

A gnat flew into my left nostril. I snorted and sneezed and it came out my right nostril. That felt weird.

"If it was me," Flash said, "I'd be shoving magazines under the seat of my jeans."

"Oh, Mom doesn't believe in spankings," Rosie said. "She'll probably just ground me for the rest of my life and make me eat peas and stuff."

"But the cats are hers, right?"

"Right."

"Gee, then I guess she'll also be kinda sad if we don't find them."

Rosie was silent for a moment. "I never really thought about that. Guess I was only thinking about me."

"You mean you were thinking about how much you're gonna get punished?"

"Not really. I was thinking about how nice it would be without those stupid cats around. But, you're right, Mom will be sad and—"

"You don't like the cats?" Flash said, as we leveled off onto a flat road that led toward the woods.

Rosie shook her head. "No, I never did. But the worst thing, Flash, is that the cats stop me from having fun."

"Huh?"

"Well, Brenda is allergic to cats."

"So am I!"

"Yeah, but Brenda's *really* allergic," Rosie said. "She's my best friend, and she can't even come over to my house to play records and stuff or she goes into a sneezing fit and gets hives and stuff. And if I

72

go over to her house, I've always gotta vacuum myself off or wear freshly cleaned clothes. I'm new in
this neighborhood, and those cats are keeping me
from seeing the only close friend I've got."

"So you don't really care if the cats come back at
all?"

Rosie shook her head. "I wish someone nice
would find them and keep them. On the other hand,
I want to play in our big game tomorrow, so I hope
we'll find them. One thing at a time, I guess. Right
now, let's see what the cat woman has to say."

We took a left and headed onto a dirt road. I
didn't know what Flash was feeling right then, but
I was pretty shocked to learn that Rosie was almost
happy the cats were gone. It got me to thinking, too.

We rode into a part of town that this dog had
never been to before. We were way past the end of
our neighborhood and back on some country road in
the woods. Every once in a while we'd pass a mailbox, but the houses were too far back in the woods
to see.

I liked it in there with all those trees, and my
nose liked all the thousands of smells. I wanted to
hop out of Flash's bike basket and romp and play
and use a bunch of those trees, but we were on a
case. Business first, trees later.

Suddenly Flash lifted his hand and stopped his
bike.

"This has to be it," he said.

We were parked next to a rusy mailbox on an old
tree stump. There was a cat painted on the mailbox
and under it was the name KATRINA BLISS.

"Where's her house?" Rosie asked, looking all
around at nothing but woods.

Flash pushed aside a few branches and pointed at

73

the ground. "I'll bet we follow this driveway here."
The driveway led into the thickest woods and disappeared.

"Well, let's get going," Rosie said.

Flash lifted me down from his bike basket, then
parked the bike next to Rosie's. We started down
the narrow path and into the woods. I smelled trees
and bushes and moss and squirrels and mice. And I
was just beginning to get a whiff of cats. A strong
whiff.

"AH-CHOO!" sneezed Flash, all over his hand.
Birds shrieked and took off. "We must be getting
close," he said.

Soon, all I could smell was cats, all kinds. We
came around a bend in the path and there was the
cat woman's house. And it was beautiful.

"Boy, for such a weird woman she—*AH-CHOO*—
sure does live in a neat house," Flash said.

Frankly, I expected some rundown spooky kind of
place, but this house looked like a cute cottage right
out of a fairy tale. It was made of stone and crooked
white planks with ivy and bright red blossoms
crawling all over it. A small stream gurgled around
its left side. I knew right away that this woman did
not cook and eat cats. Dogs maybe, but not cats.

I trotted up and took a few laps from the stream.
Ahh.

"AH-CHOO-CHOO!" Flash said. "Well, here we
go."

Flash and Rosie walked slowly toward the front
door, but before they got there, the door opened.

"They were right!" said the woman standing in
the doorway. She was tall and pretty, with black
hair and creamy white skin and bright blue eyes. I
thought she looked a little bit like Snow White, but

no one else said anything. She held a fat white cat in her arms and stroked it lovingly. Two other cats were curling themselves around her ankles.

"H-Hi," Flash said.

"My kitties are never wrong," said the woman. "They knew someone was coming, and here you are. Of course I heard you sneezing a mile away, but never mind." She looked at Rosie. "You, young woman, look familiar. Yes! The kitty litter girl! But who's the strange boy in the ridiculous green hat?"

"AH-AH-CHOO!" Flash said.

"I'm Rosie McRoy and this is Flash Fry," said Rosie.

"Pleased to meet you. You may call me Mrs. Bliss."

"Hi," said Rosie.

"CHOO-CHOO!" said Flash.

"Allergic to cats, are we?" said Mrs. Bliss. "If you have a handkerchief, Mr. Fry, you might feel better if you place it over your nose and mouth. You will sneeze much less."

"Really?" Flash said, whipping out a red-and-blue checked handkerchief. "Thank you."

Just then I stepped out of the stream to get a little attention for myself.

"Oh!" cried Mrs. Bliss. "The enemy!"

"No, no," Flash said through his handkerchief. "He's a nice dog, he likes cats, he does. His name is Scratch, and he likes cats a lot."

Mrs. Bliss hugged her white cat. More cats were around her ankles looking out at me. I guess my cute face must have got to Mrs. Bliss. "He *is* a nice-looking dog. Well, I have heard of such dogs that get along with cats, so I suppose it would be okay if he came inside."

A fat black cat appeared in the doorway and walked right out and up to me and rubbed its hairy flab against my leg.

"Tinkerbell likes him!" said Mrs. Bliss. "I've never seen anything like it. Come on in. Sodas for everyone!"

We followed Mrs. Bliss inside her house. I could tell that Flash was just as stunned as I was. The house was neat and clean. I mean, *clean*. Naturally, my super nose could smell cats all over the place, but I hardly saw any cat hairs. I wondered how that could be possible, because there were lots of cats. On the chair tops, on the mantel over the fireplace, on the windowsills, on the sofa, under the chairs... cats in all shapes and colors were slithering all around me.

And along with the cats, there were also lots of photographs and paintings of cats on the walls. On the tables and shelves were statues of cats. The throw rugs and pillows were shaped like cats. The lamps had cat lampshades. On the door was a cat calendar. I had to check myself to make sure I hadn't somehow turned into a cat. I hadn't.

"As you can plainly see," said Mrs. Bliss, returning from the kitchen with colas for Flash and Rosie and water for me, "I love cats. I love all *nice* animals, even nice doggies. But I love cats especially."

"How many do you have?" Rosie asked.

I tried talking to a couple of cats who wandered my way, but they didn't know dog language and I didn't know enough of theirs. So, I just curled up by the front door and decided to be bored and watch Flash and Rosie drink their cool sodas.

"Inside or outside?" Mrs. Bliss asked. She sat in a large green chair and two cats immediately jumped up to her lap. "You see, some are indoor cats and some are outdoor cats. All are terrific cats, but the outdoor cats love the wilderness and catch mice and birds to eat and survive. The indoor cats are more docile and lazy. Altogether? Oh, I suppose there must be fifty or so around and about."

"How did you get so many?" Flash asked.

"I'll tell you, Flash, I can't refuse a furry face," said Mrs. Bliss. "I'll give any homeless cat a home here. I'd adopt all the cats at the shelter if I could, but they won't let me have them all, poor things. But any cats who happen to wander my way and are lost, I'll take them in."

"Wow," said Rosie.

"I have names for them all," said Mrs. Bliss. "I remember them, too. That's Madeline, there's Roger and Seymour, over there is Patty, and this is Pumpernickel, on my lap are Pencil and Bear...and so forth. But today, I'm sorry to say, we are all quite sad. Two of the very first cats I ever had have gone to cat heaven."

"I'm sorry to hear that," said Flash.

"Jingles and Moxie," said Mrs. Bliss. "Old cats, they were. Husband and wife. Jingles just up and died of old age, and a few days later Moxie died of sadness. I'll miss them dearly."

A small black-and-white cat crept slowly up to my nose. I hated to admit it, but it was kind of cute. I lay perfectly still and let it sniff my nose and eyes, then it turned on its purring motor and snuggled up to my right side and fell asleep. I had to scratch my ear, but I was afraid to move.

"I must say," said Mrs. Bliss, "it certainly is nice talking to nice young people like yourselves. No one ever comes to visit me way out here in the woods. In fact, I think most people consider me to be kind of a weirdo. But I don't care. I like living alone. I've been out here for twelve years, ever since my dear husband went away."

"He died?" Rosie asked.

"No, he just went away," said Mrs. Bliss. "I never found out why, either. I don't know if he disliked the cats, or me, or what went wrong. One morning I woke up, and he was gone. Oh, well, that's old news and certainly of no interest to you kids."

Me, I was feeling kind of sorry for Mrs. Bliss. She sure had had a tough life, and now she was way out here with only her cats for company and probably very lonely. I was kind of glad we came. I sniffed the sleeping kitty at my side and it snuggled deeper into my fur.

"So, what brings you out here to see me?" asked Mrs. Bliss. The two cats on her lap were licking each other. Most of the other cats had found comfortable places to sprawl and were asleep.

"We need your help," Flash said. "It's a cat problem."

"My specialty!" she said.

"You see," Flash continued with the handkerchief over his mouth, "Rosie's three cats have mysteriously vanished."

"Oh!" said Mrs. Bliss. "I'm so very sorry to hear that."

"Thank you," Rosie said.

"So Rosie hired me to find them," Flash said. "I and a whole bunch of kids have searched the entire neighborhood, but we don't have a clue as to where they went. They've been gone all day, and we're stumped. We thought maybe you could give us some advice."

"We also thought maybe the cats might have wandered out here," Rosie said.

"Interesting, very interesting," said Mrs. Bliss. A gray cat hopped up on top of the chair and rubbed its long body back and forth along the back of her neck. She ignored it. "Well, I can tell you right off that your cats are not here. I haven't adopted any new cats in more than a month. But your problem is an interesting one, and, as you say, mysterious."

"Any ideas?" Flash asked.

"Yes and no," she said. She rose, dumping the two cats from her lap and leaving the gray cat standing puzzled on top of the chair. Mrs. Bliss paced back and forth across the room. "Now, the first thing you should realize is that cats have a strong survival instinct. What I mean by that is that they hardly ever miss a meal. They might run off, but when it is dinnertime, they come home. They are also territorial and form bonds with their owners. That means, they won't go into anyone else's home and stay there on their own. What it all boils down to is this: cats do not decide to leave home and not come back. If your cats were healthy, loved, and well fed, they might run off to play, but they should have come back."

"But Rosie's cats just moved here," said Flash.

"Well, that does change things somewhat," said Mrs. Bliss. "Yes, indeed, then perhaps the cats would have a harder time finding their way home. But, still, they could follow their own track back home. Still..."

"But what does all this mean?" asked Rosie.

"It means," said Mrs. Bliss, "that something else

79

might be responsible for the disappearance of your cats. Maybe an accident happened to all three, but I doubt it. Maybe the shelter scooped them up—did you check there?"

"Yes," said Rosie.

"Then, my young friends, that leaves only one thing. This is a case of catnapping!"

"You mean they're *asleep* somewhere?" Rosie said.

"No, silly girl," said Mrs. Bliss. "I mean someone stole them."

"Stole them!" said Rosie.

"Stole them!" said Flash.

"Stole them," said Mrs. Bliss. "It is the only solution left."

"But who would steal them?" Rosie asked.

"There are cruel people in this world," said Mrs. Bliss. "Some ride around in cars and steal animals and sell them to laboratories for horrible experiments. I have never heard of that happening around here, but it is possible. It is also possible that someone you know stole them, either because they dislike cats or as a cruel joke."

"Hmmm," Flash said. "It does appear to be the only solution left. It's something to go on, all right. Thank you, Mrs. Bliss, you've been a great help."

"A pleasure," she said. "Will you three come back to visit again sometime?"

She included me!

"Sure," said Flash.

"Thank you," Rosie said to Mrs. Bliss, then turned toward the door.

I rose, and the kitten at my side kind of flopped

over and woke with a large yawn, then scurried away. Cute.

Mrs. Bliss stood in the doorway waving to us until we were out of sight. Soon we were back at our bikes.

"She's strange, but she's nice," Flash said.

"I wonder why people think she's so weird and eats cats and everything?" Rosie asked.

"Beats me," Flash said. "I guess they don't know her. Come on, let's get going. We'll just make it home in time for dinner. Besides, I think it's going to rain any second."

Flash loaded me into his basket and we took off. Thunder rolled overhead.

"So, who stole your cats?" Flash asked.

Rosie shrugged. "I don't know, Flash. That theory sounds a little way-out to me."

"Any of your neighbors hate your cats enough to want to get rid of them?" Flash asked.

"No," Rosie said. "They have cats, too."

"Then maybe it's someone we know."

"But who'd be mean enough to do it?" Rosie asked.

"Beats me," Flash said. "Some kid, probably. Maybe somebody on the other team is trying to get you in trouble. Maybe somebody on our team is. Beats me."

"No one I know would do anything this mean, Flash. It has to be somebody on the other team."

"Unless one of your new friends doesn't like you," Flash said. "I'll think about that angle."

We reached the big hill again, but this time they had to walk their bikes up. I stayed in Flash's basket and got a free ride. As we reached the top of the hill, fat raindrops began to plop all around us and thunder shook the sky.

"We'd better get going and fast!" Flash said. "I've got plenty of work to do. I'll call you later. See you!"

"Bye, Flash," Rosie said.

And Rosie raced away on her bike toward her house, while Flash pedaled hard for our house.

By the time we got home, we were soaked. It was raining boys and girls.

Ten: Spying on the Suspect

During dinner, while Flash sat at the table with his parents and I gobbled out of a bowl on the kitchen floor, it continued to pour outside.

"Maybe it's this humid weather," said Flash's father, "but that picnic table I built sure is taking a long time to dry. I mean, it's hardly any drier now than it was this morning."

"Sure has been humid," Flash said. "I mean, *really* humid."

His father looked at him strangely, but said nothing else.

Twenty minutes later, Flash and I were downstairs in his office basement when the phone rang.

"I've got it!" Flash yelled toward the upstairs. He answered the phone.

I tuned in with my super ears to listen to the conversation.

"Flash? This is Rosie."

"Hiya, Rosie."

"Come up with anything yet?"

"Rosie, it hasn't even been an hour."

"No ideas or anything? Mom is really getting mad at me. This could be worse for me than just missing the big game. Much worse. I *have* to find those cats."

"Well, Rosie," Flash said, putting his feet up on his desk, "I do have kind of a crazy idea. A long shot, but it might turn up something."

"Anything! What is it?"

"Well, Rosie, I was thinking about Brick. How he doesn't like the team. How he doesn't like us. How he's always giving everybody trouble. I was thinking maybe it wouldn't be such a bad idea to kind of find out what he's up to."

"What do you mean?"

"I mean, it might be a good idea to go undercover, spy on him, follow him around and see where he goes. He might give us a clue. He might even lead us to the cats. Or, it might turn up nothing."

"What else can we do?" Rosie said. "Do it, Flash. You have to. We're running out of time and it's the only idea either of us has."

Flash dropped his feet to the floor and sat up. "Okay, I'll do it. It sounds like the rain is letting up. I'll leave in about fifteen minutes. It will still be light out for another hour and a half or so, but it's gloomy enough to give me some cover. I'll call you when I get back."

"Good luck."

"Thanks."

They hung up.

"Well, Scratch, time for the great detective and

his dog partner to go undercover on a dangerous mission. We have to be sneaky, boy, and we have to be quiet. But maybe—just maybe—we can crack this case. What do you think?"

I thought we were both going to get wet.

"Let's go!"

Flash went upstairs to the kitchen and, as his mother watched, puzzled, he wrapped his green hat in plastic wrap.

"Have to go outside on a case," Flash said. "Can't let my hat get wet, can I?"

"Wear your rubbers," his mother said.

"Good idea," he said. "Sneaky and quiet, too."

Before going back downstairs, Flash peeked out the window. "Good. The rain's letting up. Only drizzle now. Perfect cover."

"Bye!" Flash said to his mom.

"Don't go bringing any criminals back here," his mother laughed at him.

Downstairs again, Flash put on a dark blue nylon windbreaker. Over his sneakers he slipped black rubbers. Then he put on his plastic-wrapped hat. I laughed, but to him it sounded like a short bark.

"Okay, Scratch, be patient. Here we go."

He opened the back basement doors and we were soon outside. The rain was more like a mist. The air was warm, and even though it was still daylight, it was dim. We moved through the backyards toward Brick Glick's house. Flash walked like Groucho Marx.

We stopped behind a thick tree with a tire swing hanging from it.

"There's Brick's house," Flash whispered. "Let's have a closer look."

Flash ran up to the side of the house. His rubbers

made a slight squeaky-squishy sound on the wet grass. He flattened against the side and began to inch his way around to the front. Suddenly, the basement light went on at his feet.

Flash jumped aside and bent to peer into the window. I looked, too. Right there, two feet from us, was Brick Glick. His back was to us and he was searching for something in a box. Then he turned and raised his face. Flash quickly fell back from the window, breathing heavily. A few seconds later the basement light went off.

"Did he see us, boy?" Flash whispered. "Please, tell me he didn't see us. We'll just have to wait and see what happens."

Minutes went by. I used them to water the bushes.

"I don't think he saw us," Flash whispered. "Let's go around front."

We snuck around the front of the house, and Flash peered carefully in the front window. Brick was putting on his coat and saying something to his mother.

"He's coming out!" Flash whisper-screamed. "Back around the side!" He scurried around the side of the house.

A minute later, Brick Glick came through his front door. He popped open an umbrella and started walking quickly down the sidewalk. Flash stayed about twenty yards behind Brick. While Brick walked down the sidewalk, Flash stumbled and splashed through bushes and over lawns.

Brick then took a left, cut between two houses, and headed back toward the woods. Flash frowned, wondering where Brick could be going. But Flash had no choice; he had to follow him.

Moving from tree to tree and rock to rock, Flash followed Brick into the soggy woods, down a muddy path, over a rushing stream, then back down the path and out of the woods. Now we were in the park.

"Where is he going?" Flash whispered. "This could be good, Scratch!"

Brick calmly walked the winding pathway through the park, past the wet and empty benches and dripping stone barbecues, and across the huge, mud-puddly parking lot. Flash had a hard time keeping up, diving behind benches and trees and sloshing through puddles, but he managed to keep Brick in sight. Me, I just jogged along. The wetness felt good on my fur and my feet, and the fresh mud puddles were great to lap, and there were plenty of worms to sniff.

Then Brick was back on the sidewalk again. He walked along for a few minutes, then crossed the street and headed for a row of lighted buildings.

The first building Brick came to was a barber shop. It was closed. Brick walked up to the pay phone that was there and felt in the slot for change. He found nothing. Then Brick walked to the next store, a deli, which was open, peered in the window, then opened the door and went inside. Flash hugged close to the wall and waited.

A few minutes later, Brick came out and turned left—right toward Flash!

Flash quickly sidestepped along the wall, around the corner, then ran through two mud puddles, dove over a bush, and flattened out behind it on the soaking wet grass. He was a mess. Me, I was having fun, prancing along beside Flash, nipping at his socks, and lying down beside him and licking his cheeks. Flash didn't think I was cute at all.

Brick walked past us and kept going for about ten yards. Then he stopped, turned around, and walked past us again, past the barber shop and deli, toward the next store.

"That was close!" Flash whispered. "But what the heck is he doing?"

Flash stood up. He was soaking wet. The front of his shirt and jeans were coated with water, mud, and grass clippings. He put his finger to his lips and said *"Shhh"* to me, then snuck up to the buildings again and followed along behind Brick, this time farther back.

"He's going to Gumm's," Flash said. He ducked low, ran out to the curb, and hid behind a parked car that had a good view of the store. I trotted along behind him. I sniffed at the car's right rear tire. Kong had been there.

Gumm's Candy Store was a place most kids like to go. Not only did they have the best selection of candy in the world, but you could sit there and have a milkshake or a soda and nobody would kick you out for just hanging around. Sure enough, Brick went inside.

Flash crouched down low. "I wonder how long he'll be in there? Minutes? Hours?" He shivered. "Sure is colder out here when you're wet."

The minutes ticked by.

"I have to see what's going on in there," Flash said. "What if he's meeting a friend in there? Maybe a friend who knows where the cats are? What if he's meeting someone from the other team? *Shhhh*."

Flash did his Groucho walk very slowly to the next car up, then the next car, until he was directly in front of Gumm's. He rose up and peered over the top of the hood. I stood on my hind legs and peered with him.

The only person we could see was the kid behind the counter. The store was empty.

"Maybe Brick's in the bathroom," Flash said.

We stood there a few more minutes, and Brick didn't come out of the bathroom.

"Where is he?" Flash said.

"He's right behind you!"

"Yaaa!" Flash whirled around, slipped, and fell on his butt into a huge mud puddle. "Brick!"

Brick bent over laughing. "Scared you, huh?"

"But—"

"Some detective you are!" Brick said. "I snuck out the back door of Gumm's and snuck up on you!"

Flash stood up, dripping and embarrassed.

"Have fun following me around, creep?" Brick asked.

"I'm not...I mean, I..."

"Forget it, Flash. I saw you looking in my basement window at home and decided to have a little fun," Brick said. "Wet out here, isn't it?"

For once, Flash was speechless. I'm sure he felt like a jerk. I know I felt like a jerk for him.

"Serves you right for spying on people," Brick said. Then he got serious. "You think I have the cats, right? Isn't that why you're following me? Huh?"

Flash didn't say anything. He just stood there and dripped.

"Well," Brick said, "it figures. Listen, Flash, I know you and the rest of the team are jealous because I'm the best baseball player on the team. Everybody always gives me a hard time because I'm better than the rest of you, that's why none of you can understand how *stupid* I feel losing game after game after game. I belong on a *good* team! And if we don't play and get killed tomorrow, I'll be *happy!* Get it? Now, I don't want you bothering me anymore. Just stay away. Go chase your kitty-cats, but leave me alone."

"Brick," Flash said, "you've got it wrong. Okay, maybe I thought maybe you had the cats. And maybe I'm wrong and a stinking detective. But the team needs you, Brick. We want you *with* us, not against us."

For a moment, I thought maybe Brick was about to say something nice. But then he frowned, waved his hand, and said, "Foo!"

And Brick stormed off down the wet street.

"Darn," Flash said, leaning back against the car. "Well, there goes the case. If he's got the cats, we'll never know now. Not only have I failed at the case and let the whole team down, but Brick will hate me forever, and it'll probably ruin my whole detective career. Darn."

Boy, I wished I could talk to Flash right then. I really did. Because I wasn't ready to give up. Sure, Brick caught Flash spying on him, but so what? Flash isn't the only member of this detective team. There's me, Scratch, Private Nose.

Maybe Flash was out of clues, out of ideas, and out of hope. But not old Scratch. No, sir. Old Scratch had a few more tricks left up his nose, because something good did come out of this embarrassing night, and I really, really wished I could tell Flash what it was.

Because, while Brick was giving his speech to Flash, I put my super detective nose to work. And I smelled something on Brick's hand that could break this case wide open. What did I smell? Cat food, folks, *cat food!*

And Brick doesn't have any cats! At least he doesn't have any cats that are his own, that is.

Eleven: A Cat Chat with Dogs

Flash was silent all the way home. He just dripped and squished and slumped. His mother and father yelled at him for being soaking wet, but he didn't even care. He just mumbled he was sorry, stripped off his wet clothes, and shuffled up to his room in his underwear. He was embarrassed and beaten.

Me, I was just starting to fight. I'd get Flash out of this fix if it was the last thing I did. Actually, I hoped it wasn't the last thing I did. Really, I wished it would be the *next* thing I did. Anyway.

It was a little after eight o'clock and getting dark outside. Flash was watching TV in his bathrobe like a sick kid. His father was snoring in his easy chair, and Flash's mother was doing a crossword puzzle. It was time to take myself for a walk.

I trotted down to the basement, lifted the back door latch with my nose, gave the door a shove with my paw. The door swung open and out I went. I closed the door behind me. If the door had been locked, it would have been much trickier. But it wasn't, so who cares.

It was still drizzling out, but since I'm a dog I loved it. I snuffled it, I rolled in it, and I licked it. Then I ran through five backyards to visit a really good friend of mine. A girl. A girl dog, that is.

Her name is Marzipan. She's a frisky Irish setter with gorgeous red hair and big brown eyes. We'd almost fallen in love once a while back, but that was before the human she lives with fenced in her backyard. Now she has to stay inside the fence like a prisoner, and it's harder to get in and see her, though I have my ways.

When I ran up to the fence she started swishing her gorgeous long tail so hard that she almost fell over.

"Scratchie!" she said.

"Hi, cute nose," I said.

"Scratchie," she sighed. "You never visit much anymore."

I shrugged. "It's hard having a girlfriend in a cage."

"But not impossible," she said.

"No," I said, "not impossible."

"Come here, gimme a kiss, Scratchie."

I poked my nose through the fence and licked her front teeth. She licked mine, then rubbed my nose with hers. Wow! What a girl!

We were talking the way dogs always talk: with body language and sign language. Every tilt of the head, squat, prance, lift of an eyebrow, wag of a tail means something. Like I said earlier, it's complicated—unless you're a dog. Marzi could communicate very well.

"Someday, Scratchie, you'll have to bust me out of this yard. Then we can run away together and never come back."

"Who'd feed us?" I asked, suddenly afraid. "I mean, I'm not much of a hunter."

"And you're not very romantic, either," she said with a woof. "Oh, Scratchie, I suppose you are on another case, right? That's the only reason you come to visit me anymore."

"It is not," I said. "I came over here tonight to, to...well, to see you. But first, now that you mention it, I do happen to be involved in a slight investigation. I need your help, Marzi."

"You do?" She danced around in a little circle. "You really want me to help? Oh, I love it when you want me to help with your detecting. What? What can I do?"

What a dog, what a gorgeous dog! She's perfect for me! Perfect! So perfect, it's a crime! Well, that was almost funny, wasn't it?

I gave her my serious detective dog look. "Have you seen...any cats around here lately? Specifically...The Three Stooges, Rosie McRoy's cats?"

"The new girl? No, I haven't seen them, Scratchie," Marzi said.

"Darn."

"But I have heard them."

"Heard them? You have?" I said, almost barking out loud.

"Yes, I'm pretty sure it was them."

"Okay, Marzi, lemme have the whole story."

"Sure," she said, "as soon as you hop over the fence."

"What!"

"I'm not going to tell you a thing, Scratchie, unless you come over here with me. I've missed you!"

"Oh, no!" I said. "Business first."

"I mean business!" she said.

I guess she did. I checked around to make sure no one was watching, then walked to the lowest part of the fence and leapt up, got my paws over the top, pumped my back legs like crazy, and plopped over into Marzi's yard.

She was on me in a second, licking my front teeth and rubbing noses.

"Okay, okay!" I said, giggling. "This mystery is very important. Flash's whole career is on the line, not to mention his big game."

"You sure are loyal to your master," she huffed. "I wish you were that loyal to me."

"Give me time," I said. "Now, what about the cats? What did you mean when you said you *heard* them?"

"Just that. I heard them. They were in a box."

"A box?"

"Yes."

I sighed. "Mind explaining that a little, Marzi?"

"It was a cardboard box, and Rosie's cats were inside. I knew they were Rosie's cats because I've heard Rosie's cats before, and these were them."

"And?"

"And what?"

"And what else, Marzi? Tell me the whole story."

"Oh, okay. This moring a cat scream woke me up. I listened some more and heard The Three Stooges screaming from inside a cardboard box from the woods behind your house."

Remember, Marzi is a dog. Even though the cats were five houses away, her keen ears could still hear them and her sharp nose could still smell the cardboard box. If Marzi was a human, she wouldn't have known what the heck was going on.

"Then," Marzi continued, "I heard human breathing and human footsteps. Then I heard a clank, and I knew the cats were put into a metal cage of some kind."

"Who was the human?" I asked.

"Brick Glick. I'd smell him a mile away."

"Hmmmmmm," I said by showing only my top front teeth.

Sooooooo, Brick Glick nabbed the cats after Flash chucked them in the woods this morning, eh!

"Anything else?" I asked.

"Yes. Then Brick Glick picked up the cage and walked away with it. I didn't hear where he went because my master called me in for food."

"You did great, Marzi, really, really great. I'm proud of you!"

"I did? You are?"

"I've gotta go."

"Scratchie!"

"Sorry, but you just gave me the information to blow this case wide open. And I need all the time I can get to figure out how to do it. But don't worry, I'll be back."

"Promise?" she whined.

"I promise."

"I'll miss you until then, Scratchie," she said, licking my nose.

I licked hers a few times. "Same here." I don't

know why humans don't lick each other's noses. It feels great, and tastes even better! "Bye for now."

"Good-bye, and good luck on your case, cutie!"

I blushed. "Thanks."

I crawled up and over the fence and raced off toward the woods. Ahhhh. She loves me.

It was dark out now and still drizzly. I smashed through bushes and jumped over logs, with my nose to the ground the whole time. Soon, I picked up the scent of cats and heard their faint meowing. I knew I'd missed their scent earlier because I'd gone the wrong way! But now, I was closing in.

I was quite a bit past my house when I saw them. Curly, Larry, and Moe were crammed into a cage out behind Brick Glick's house. When I came up to the cage the cats cowered in a corner. The cage had a metal roof, so the cats were dry. Piled in a heap to the left were empty cat food cans—the same brand I smelled on Brick earlier. At least the jerk fed them.

Now what?

Somehow, I had to talk to these cats. But they were still cowering, afraid of me, the big bad doggie. I got around to where they could get a good look at my cute face, and I dropped an ear, hung out my tongue, and lay down with my paws over my nose.

They laughed.

That was a start. I did the same thing again, smiling.

They laughed again, then Curly, the black one with the white nose, began walking slowly back and forth, rubbing his side against the cage and purring in this weird way. He was trying to talk to me, but what was he saying? I watched as Curly did it again. Then I got it! I remembered once an old wise dog telling me that cats communicate mostly by contact. I didn't know what it meant then, but I had a good idea of what it meant now. He wanted me to let him out!

I touched the door of the cage with my paw, and Curly touched it with his cheek. That's it!

But it wasn't enough. I had to communicate a message to them, because they were about to play a big role in exposing this whole mystery. I put my great mind to work. But nothing worked. I was just sitting there in the rain, with the mystery practically solved, and I was stumped as to how to finish it because I couldn't talk to cats!

"Are you, by any chance, trying to talk to us?" said Moe, the orange cat, with body and sign language.

"Yes," I said, "but I don't know how to talk to you."

"Too bad," said Larry.

"Yes, isn't it," said Curly.

"Pity," said Moe.

Then they all laughed.

Finally, I caught on. "Hey! You're talking dog language!"

"Let that be a lesson to you!" said Curly. "Cats *are* smarter than dogs. We can talk cat language *and* dog language. That proves we're smarter! So there!"

I just looked at them. "You're smarter, huh? So how come you're the ones in the cage?"

They stopped laughing.

"Forget it," I said. "I have a new respect for cats, and I am really glad we can talk. How would you like to get back at the creep who put you in this cage?"

"Yes!" They all said.

"First," I said, "it is very important for you to be taken back home by my human master, Flash Fry."

"Fine with us," said Moe. "We like him. Silly hat, but a nice boy."

"Good," I said. "Here's the plan. I let you out, you follow me back to my house, we all pretend Flash discovers you, and he takes you home."

"Perfect!" said The Three Stooges.

But just as I was working on the cage's latch with my teeth, Brick Glick showed up.

"Hey! Hey, mutt!" he screamed. "Beat it! Shoo!"

I didn't shoo. I had to get this latch open! With my lips, teeth, and paws I worked from every angle as Brick ran toward us through the wet bushes.

Clank. The latch fell, and the door swung open.

"This way!" I yelled.

And I took off, with The Three Stooges right behind me. We ducked under bushes and scooted around rocks, and ran in circles until we had completely baffled Brick Glick and were free to run to my house. That was a close one.

Once we were in my backyard I asked the cats if they'd wait a minute. Somehow I had to get Flash out here to "discover" them.

"Sure," said Larry. "We've got a lot of stretching to catch up on."

I let myself in the back door and closed it behind me. I padded down into the basement. I walked over to a corner where Flash's father had some drop cloths stacked, pulled one off, and rolled around on it until I was pretty dry. Then I went upstairs to Flash.

He was sitting in front of the TV like a zombie.

This was one sad detective boy. I barked three times and pranced around in front of him.

"Have to go out, Scratch?"

I pranced and barked.

"You sure?"

I barked and pranced.

"Oh, all right. Just a minute."

Slowly, he slid into his slippers. Then, like a kid in cement jeans walking through waist-high glue, he shuffled to the basement to let me out the back door.

"Worst day of my life, worst day of my life," he kept muttering.

Poor Flash. Don't worry, Flash, your luck is about to change.

Soon, he opened the back door and I burst through.

"Don't be too long," he said. But he didn't look outside at the three cats who were just sitting there staring at him.

I barked. He didn't look. I barked again. Nothing.

I turned to Curly. "Can't you meow, or something?"

Curly, Larry, and Moe started meowing like crazy. That got Flash's attention in a hurry.

"Hey...Well...Holy cow...Wow, I don't believe it!" said Flash.

I'd never seen him move faster. In a wink, he was outside and had The Three Stooges in his arms.

"*AH-CHOO!* This is great! *AH-HA-CHOO!* I've got Rosie's cats! Oh, boy! *AH-CHOOOOOO!*"

Ten minutes later, with Flash sneezing up a storm, he and I and the three cats were standing on

104

Rosie's doorstep. Flash had told his parents he'd just found Rosie's Mom's lost cats and he'd be back soon. They were proud of him. Now, Rosie herself answered the door.

"Flash! Oh, Flash! You found Mom's cats," Rosie said, gathering the cats in her arms. "Mom! Mom! Flash found the cats!" I heard her mother getting up in the living room. "Oh, boy, Flash, now I can play in the big game!"

Flash was all smiles. *"AH-CHOO!"* he said.

Soon, Mrs. McRoy appeared at the door. "Flash Fry, you little detective, you. Thank you very much for finding my cats. Where on earth were they?"

"I—*AH-CHOO!*—don't know where they've been," said Flash, "but I found them wandering around my backyard. I nabbed them right away."

"Well, you did good, young man," said Rosie's mom. "Poor Rosie here has been so worried, I think she's learned her lesson about keeping her eye on them."

"I sure have," Rosie said, not altogether happy with taking the blame.

"I think this deserves a reward," said Rosie's mother.

"Not so fast," said a voice from behind her. An older woman stepped into view.

"What?" said Rosie's mom.

"Hello, Flash," said Mrs. Wain. It was the woman who'd given Flash the reward for returning her cats.

"AH-AH-CHOO! Hello, Mrs. Wain," said Flash, kind of puzzled because Mrs. Wain didn't look all that friendly.

Mrs. Wain addressed Rosie's mother. "Isn't it strange," she said. "Flash here returned my cats only today, and I gave him a nice reward. And here he is returning your cats and getting a reward, too."

"What do you mean?" asked Rosie's mom.

"Well," said Mrs. Wain, "isn't it a bit strange that Flash is finding all the lost cats around here? Seems to me he's got a nice little business going here. In fact, he tried to return my cats once more for a reward!"

"I didn't want any reward," Flash said. "And I don't want one now."

Mrs. McRoy gave Flash a mean stare. "I'd say it is pretty lucky I asked Mrs. Wain for dinner tonight. Where have you been hiding my cats?"

"I haven't!" Flash cried, holding back another sneeze.

"And how many other cats do you have? You catnapper!" asked Mrs. Wain.

"Flash didn't do it!" Rosie screamed. "I know he didn't!"

"I never did trust him, him and his weird green hat," said Mrs. McRoy.

"You should have seen him snatch that money right out of my hand," said Mrs. Wain. "Then he has the nerve to try it again!"

"Why are you picking on me?" Flash said. He was near tears now. "I didn't steal your cats."

"Well, cats don't just go off on their own, do they?" said Rosie's mother. "No, they do not. Good night!"

And she slammed the door in Flash's face.

If only dogs could talk. If only I could tell everyone that Brick Glick was to blame, and that Flash was a good guy for returning Mrs. Wain's cats when he didn't have to. I guess they'd rather blame Flash. This was horrible.

"This is horrible," said Flash, moving slowly down the steps, wiping tears from his eyes. "I crack the case and end up being the villain."

I walked close to Flash's leg the whole way home. Flash's father was waiting for him.

"Son, I just got a call from Mrs. McRoy," he said. "She says you stole her cats, then tried to return them to her for money."

"I didn't!" he cried, almost sobbing now. "Her cats have been missing all day. I-I found them in the backyard. I-I brought them b-back and she offered me money. Then that Mrs. Wain called me a cat-napper because I found her cats earlier today and brought them back to her and she gave me money. S-so Mrs. McRoy thinks...oh, I didn't do anything!" And he broke down crying.

I curled up at his feet and licked his ankles. He stroked my ear. One of his tears dripped onto my nose and I licked it away. It was salty and sad.

"I believe you," said Flash's dad. He gave Flash a big hug. "I know all the good cases you've solved. You're a good kid and I know they're mistaken. I also know that Mrs. McRoy was very upset about her missing cats. I'll give her a call later and calm her down."

"Th-thanks, Dad," Flash said.

Later, when Flash was tucked in bed and I was curled up down at the bottom, he said: "Worst day of my life. I solve a case, find the cats, get Rosie back on the team, but my career is ruined. Tomorrow, Mrs. McRoy will tell the whole neighborhood I stole her cats for money. There's no way out."

The worst part was it looked like Brick Glick got away with the whole thing.

Flash went to sleep sad.

But I couldn't sleep at all. I had a great idea cooking in my mind. And since I couldn't sleep, I quietly got up, wrapped a bunch of doggie treats I'd been keeping for emergencies into a small drop cloth, and ran out the back door and into the night. Soon I jumped up and over the fence into Marzipan's yard. Luckily, she was outside and very glad to see me.

Twelve: Cat Case Cracked

Later that night, on my way home from Marzipan's house, I wound my way past Rosie's. I was in luck. The Three Stooges were outside. I hugged close to the house beneath the kitchen window in case Mrs. McRoy happened to look out.

"Hi, guys," I said to them. "Pretend I'm not here."

"Gotcha," said Moe.

"Tough break for your master," said Curly.

"What's up?" asked Larry.

"It's about my master," I said. "I'd like you to please do me one more favor."

"Sure! Anything for the dog who got us out of that terrible cage," said Moe. The others agreed.

"Great," I said. "Now listen. Tomorrow afternoon, at about twelve o'clock..."

* * *

The next day, Sunday, burst sunny and glittering and warm. But all morning, Flash Fry moped around and was the saddest kid detective on earth. The big game was supposed to take place at one o'clock, but he wasn't even excited, even though Rosie was going to be pitching.

"It's just no fun solving a case and being blamed for *causing* the case!" he said.

Even his mother and father tried to cheer him up but couldn't. No, nobody in the world could cheer up poor Flash Fry. Except me. *If* my plan worked.

At twelve o'clock, with the sun burning bright overhead, Flash Fry, Private Eye and so-so first basemen, walked onto the baseball field in his pink-and-white uniform and met the rest of the Pink Bunny Lasers, who were there an hour early for a warm-up practice. The Lucky Laundry Tornadoes weren't there yet.

Flash's whole team cheered when they saw him.

"All right, Flash is here!" yelled Curtis. "The guy who saved the day by finding the cats and getting us our secret weapon pitcher back!"

Mr. Slith, whose white baseball pants were too short for him so his hairy legs were sticking out, grabbed Flash's hand and shook it. "Way to go, Flash. Now we have a chance, I feel it in my bones."

"We're gonna kill the Tornadoes, right, Flash?" said Pete.

"Yeah, sure," Flash said.

"Looks like Flashie's gonna start crying," Brick said. "Defeat must be in the wind."

"Uh-oh," said Pete. "Team, huddle! We've got a problem here."

The whole team gathered around Flash Fry, who

sat down on the ground. I curled up at his feet. He rubbed my head gloriously.

"What's the matter with him?" asked Marybeth.

"I don't know," said Gene. "Maybe we'd better ask him."

"Good idea," said Brenda. "Flash, why are you acting so weird?"

Flash just shrugged.

"I know why," said Rosie. And she explained to the team how Flash got blamed for catnapping her cats and asking for money.

"So what? Who cares?" said Curtis. "You got Rosie here and that's all that matters."

"That's all that matters?" Flash said angrily. "No way! I'm out of business if I don't clear my name. This is the worst thing that ever happened to me. And what makes it worse is that I'm innocent!"

"Well, what can we do?" Gene said.

"There must be something we can do to help our hero," said Mr. Slith.

"Yeth, Mr. Slith, there mutht be," said Pete.

"Why don't we just—" began Brick Glick.

"You shut up!" screamed Rosie. "You didn't even help us look for my cats, you creep. So you just shut up!"

"Why pick on me?" asked Brick.

Just then, a small red car drove up and stopped with a screech. Rosie's mother got out and stormed up.

"My cats!" she yelled. "They're gone again! Flash Fry, where are they?"

"Hey, you can't blame me again!" Flash said.

This was my cue to go into action. I started prancing and barking around Flash like a crazy dog.

111

"What's with your dog, Flash?" asked Pete.

"What is it, boy?" asked Flash. A brief glimmer came into his eyes. *He knows that when I prance like this, I mean business.*

I ran away and came back, ran away and came back.

"He wants us to follow him!" Flash said, leaping to his feet.

"Are you nuts?" Curtis said. "How do you know that?"

"I know," said Flash. "You can stay here if you want to, but I'm following my loyal partner!"

"Partner?" said Gene.

"What about the game!" screamed Marybeth.

"There's time until the game," said Pete to his sister. "But you stay here. If the other team comes before we get back, stall them. I've seen Scratch do this before, and when he does, it always means something."

"Oh, all right," said Marybeth, sitting down to wait.

I took off. And everybody, including Rosie's mother, who wouldn't stop yelling at Flash, sprinted after me.

Brick Glick, who is a very fast runner, was right up beside me, bumping me away from the path I wanted to go on. Gee, I wonder why? I was going toward his house!

Zoom! I led everyone right up the side of Brick's house and into the woods. There was the cage. And there, inside the cage, were The Three Stooges.

Not bad, eh? Let me pause here and explain what I did. It's really pretty simple. I couldn't let Flash suffer and Brick Glick get away with catnapping the cats. I had to somehow expose Brick Glick as

112

the villain. Then I got the idea: if I could somehow catch Brick with the cats, that would prove beyond a shadow of a doubt he stole them.

Last night, after my romantic late-night picnic with Marzipan, I'd asked the cats to sneak out and go back into the cage at around twelve o'clock. Then I would lead everyone over so we could find the cats in Brick's cage, and see the empty cat food cans, and put two and two together and realize Brick was the catnapper and not Flash. It was a simple plan and it worked perfectly. Almost.

"Flash Fry!" said Rosie's mother, all out of breath. "Why did you steal my cats again and put them in this cage?"

Well, Flash had had enough of Mrs. McRoy. You can only push Flash so far before he sticks up for his rights.

"Why are you picking on me?" he yelled at her. "Why do you think *I* put your cats in this cage? Can't you see the cage is in *Brick's* yard? What do you have against me? Can't you tell when I'm trying to do something *good* for you and Rosie?"

"Well, I..." was all Mrs. McRoy could say for the moment. She bent, opened the cage, and scooped her three squirming cats into her arms. Then she handed Moe to Rosie.

"What are these cats doing back here?" said Brick Glick. His eyes were wide and his mouth was open.

Boy, Brick must have been really confused. Last night, he'd seen me running away with the cats. And now, suddenly the cats were back in the cage! This was great!

"Well, I..." Mrs. McRoy was still trying to talk. "Well, if you're not to blame, Flash, who is?"

113

Everyone, and I mean even the bugs and the trees and the worms, said: "BRICK!" Brick was now looking like the guiltiest boy in the world.

"Really?" said Rosie's mom. "It wasn't Flash? Why not? I mean, Mrs. Wain said...I mean...oh, I don't know what I mean! But if it was you, Mr. Glick, you'd better start talking!"

Brick looked like he was thinking about running, but we had him surrounded.

"Okay, okay, okay, okay," Brick said. "I want to be a professional baseball player, see? But what happens? I'm stuck on an *un*professional team that has stinko players and loses every single game they play. It's embarrassing. Not only that, I have to wear this stupid pink-and-white uniform. What professional baseball team has pink-and-white uniforms? And now we have to play the best team in the league, the Tornadoes, and all my friends are on the team. I can play as good as they can, but here I am doomed to lose to them! I just couldn't take it anymore. I wanted to quit the team, but my parents gave me a big lecture about quitters. I had to think of some way to get out of playing this game. So, when I heard that Rosie couldn't play if her cats weren't found, and when Flash told us where he saw them in the woods, I left and found the cats and stuck them in the cage. That way, we wouldn't have enough players and we'd have to forfeit the game. Mr. Slith told us that no team could play with eight players. You have to forfeit, and the other team wins automatically."

"You sneak!" cried Rosie, red-as-a-beet mad.

"Well, it's better than losing and looking like a bunch of jerks!" said Brick. "I figured I'd let the cats

114

loose after we forfeited the game and no one would know I took them."

"I'm confused," said Gene. "Flash found the cats last night in his backyard, and returned them. How did you steal them the second time?"

Brick looked mystified. "But I *didn't!* Last night, the cats escaped. I came out here and saw Scratch at the cage, and then the cats were running away. That dumb mutt somehow must have gotten them out of the cage. But he certainly couldn't have gotten them back in."

"Who cares how it happened—the important thing is that Flash is innocent!" said Pete.

"Not...so...fast," said Rosie's mother. Her face was all scrunched up, she was thinking so hard. "Maybe Scratch chased the cats into Flash's backyard last night. But how did *my* cats *happen* to get into *Flash's* house yesterday morning in the first place? Huh? Brick didn't do that."

"I didn't!" Brick said.

"Flash?" said Mrs. McRoy. "I smell something fishy."

"Not fishy, meaty," Flash said. "I must have been right yesterday when I figured the cats had gotten a sniff of Scratch's dog food and followed the scent in to my basement! And that's just where I found them."

"Okay, but what were the cats doing so far away from our house in the first place?" asked Rosie's mother.

"I...Um...I..." Flash said.

"Well?" said Mrs. McRoy.

"I did it!" shouted Rosie. "I dumped them in the woods behind Flash's house!"

115

We were all stunned. We looked at Rosie in total shock.

"I couldn't take it anymore, Mom," Rosie cried. "I hated having cats that kept my best friend Brenda away from my house because she's allergic to them. I'm lonely, so I did it! I dropped them into the woods by Flash's house. I figured that since it's a new neighborhood for them, they couldn't find their way home. I hoped maybe they'd wander to someone else's house, and maybe they'd feed them and keep them and give them a nice home. Anyway, as soon as I let them go, I knew I made a big, dumb mistake. It was a horrible thing to do to cats. So I went back to look for them, but they were gone! I guess by then they had already followed the smell of Scratch's food and gotten into Flash's basement. It was awful when you said I couldn't play in the big game until I found them, and everyone was so much help, and..." Rosie started crying. "I'm sorry!"

Nobody said anything. We all looked to Rosie, who was bawling. Then we looked to Flash, who was frowning. Then we looked to Brick, who was kind of pale. Then we looked to Rosie's mom, who was just then moving in to hug her daughter.

"I didn't know how much you hated The Three Stooges," she said.

"I...don't hate them," said Rosie. "I just don't like them living with us. I want to have fun with *humans*."

Just then Marybeth ran up. "The Tornadoes are waiting! They say if you're not back there in two minutes, we forfeit and they win the game."

"Go on," Rosie's mom said. "Give me Moe and go on out there and play your game! And win!"

"Let's go, Lasers!" cried Mr. Slith.

116

We all ran at top speed to the baseball field. The Lucky Laundry Tornadoes were there, looking sharp in their brilliant blue-and-yellow uniforms, smartly tossing the ball back and forth like rockets.

"We're here! We're here!" called Mr. Slith.

There was no grandstand at the field, so the people who came to watch brought lawn chairs and blankets. Flash's parents were there, waving and smiling. Most of the other parents were there, too. Even my good dogfriend Kong was there with Brenda's folks. But Brick's parents weren't there. He'd probably told them not to come.

"Hey, Brick!" called one of the Tornadoes. "Nice bunny uniforms! Why don't you hop out onto the field?" Their whole team laughed and called some more insults.

Brick didn't answer. He just turned red and gritted his teeth.

The umpire came over. "You're six minutes late. Mind if we start the game?"

"No, let's go, let's go," said Mr. Slith. "Okay, Lasers, let's go! Take the field!"

"No," Brick said.

We all stopped in our tracks.

"No!" he said again. He dropped his glove. "I'm *not playing!*"

117

Thirteen: Dog Attack!

"WHAT!" said all of the Lasers.

"I'm not playing," Brick said again. He suddenly bent over at the waist. "I . . . I've got a stomachache. A really bad one. And I feel kind of dizzy. I think I'm gonna throw up soon."

Flash stormed up in front of Brick. "After all I've gone through, you're not playing? After all that everybody has gone through, you're quitting at the last minute? After a whole season of playing our guts out, we don't even test ourselves against the best team?"

"I told you, I'm sick!"

"Ha!" said Flash. "The only place you're sick, Brick, is in the head!"

The whole team started yelling at Brick, and I really think that Flash would have jumped him if Mr. Slith didn't step in.

"Take it easy, Flash," said Mr. Slith. "Maybe we can work this thing out."

"I . . . I have to go home," said Brick. He slowly rose, and we all watched as he shuffled away. He was crying, but I think I was the only one short enough to see the tears on his downturned face.

Mr. Slith motioned for the umpire and for the Tornadoes to meet him on the pitcher's mound. Both teams walked out onto the field and huddled.

"What's going on?" demanded the umpire.

"We've got a sick player," said Mr. Slith. "He had to go home. That leaves us with only eight players. How about we play the game anyway?"

The coach of the Tornadoes shook his head, but it was the umpire who spoke. "You know the rules. Everyone plays with nine players. You don't have nine, you forfeit and the other team wins by default."

"Looks like it's all over," said Rosie.

"Gee," said one of the guys on the Tornadoes, "you Lasers were easier to beat than we thought!"

"Awww," said another Tornado, "I was looking forward to beating their little pink bunny tails off!"

"Knock it off!" shouted Curtis.

Soon, everyone was shouting at everyone else.

Me, I had an idea and I was going nuts. I took off running around and around the whole group, barking and yipping like crazy. I stopped and sat there panting when Pete started hollering.

"Hold it down! Hold it down!" Pete yelled. Everyone hushed up. "We *do* have nine players!"

"You do?" said the Tornado coach.

"We do?" said all the Lasers.

"Sure," said Pete, with a little smile. "We've got

120

Flash, Rosie, Curtis, Brenda, George, Gene, Mary-beth, me, and Scratch."

"Scratch?" said one of the Tornadoes. "Who's Scratch?"

"Him!" Pete said. He was pointing at me.

"A *dog?*" said the umpire.

The Tornadoes all stood there with their mouths hanging open. I looked up at them and wagged my stubby tail.

"Pete," said Marybeth, "this is no time for one of your stupid jokes."

"It's not a joke!" Flash said.

"Huh?" Pete said.

"Yeah!" Flash said. "Why not? Scratch can play. Watch this!" Flash picked up a baseball and tossed it in the air in my direction. I scurried under it, waited, then caught it cleanly in my chops. I trotted it back to Flash.

The Tornadoes were still getting a big kick out of the whole idea. "Great, so the pooch can retrieve a ball," said one of them. "But how can a dog bat? Huh?"

Flash said, "That's our problem, isn't it? So, do we play or not?"

The Tornado coach, smiling like crazy, shrugged and said, "Ump?"

The umpire rolled his eyes and said: "PLAY BALL!"

It was a dream come true. After all my hours of playing ball with Flash, after being a baseball fan for years, the rookie dog gets his big break.

Mr. Slith had an extra white-and-pink baseball jersey, and they slipped my front legs into it and pulled it over my head.

"Go get 'em, Scratch!" said a few of the Lasers.

When I trotted out onto the field, all the people on the sidelines cheered and waved. I noticed that Miss Bliss was now among them. Kong was barking like a maniac. I took my position in center field, while the first Tornado batter stepped up to the plate.

Rosie was pitching for our team. All the Lasers were chanting at her to strike them out. She wound up and fired the first pitch.

"Steeeeerike!" cried the umpire.

We all cheered. I barked. I had a good view from center field. I could see that the batter was standing a little too close to the plate. That meant that a good inside pitch would be the best to throw—hard to hit, and even if he hit it, it would be weak. Rosie, though, fired one outside.

Crack! went the bat, and the ball came screaming out to me on two fast hops. I bolted to my right, snagged the ball in my jaws, sprinted to the short-stop, Brenda, who had come out to meet me, and she fired the ball in to second.

The crowd went nuts. Some of the smiles on the Tornadoes weakened a little. I was a big-time player.

The next batter hit a slow one to the second base-man, Curtis. He threw it to Brenda, who moved to touch second, and she threw it to Flash at first.

"Double play!" yelled Flash. "Our first double play of the year!"

"Yippee!" shouted Mr. Slith, acting more like a little kid than a coach. "Everything is coming together now! You really look like a baseball team now!"

The next batter walked. The next batter whacked a good one. It flew so high it looked like a marble.

122

But I was under it. I could catch it, naturally, but if I did it would probably knock out all my teeth. I had to think of something else. The ball rocketed down, and I let it hit the ground right in front of me.

"The dumb dog missed it!" I heard someone on the Tornadoes yell.

I grabbed the ball in my teeth and took off as fast as my four legs could carry me. I flew onto the infield and zoomed over second base just before the guy who was running from first could get there.

"Runner's out!" cried the umpire. "Lasers are up!"

That really drove the crowd crazy.

I dropped the ball on the pitcher's mound and trotted in with the rest of the team. On the bench, all the Lasers ruffled my hair and patted my back. I licked everybody's hand.

"Flash," said Mr. Slith, "how's Scratch going to bat?"

Flash looked worried. "I haven't figured that out yet."

Mr. Slith nodded, then he addressed the team. "Okay, team! You're looking great out there, the best ever! And I mean *ever!* Let's get mad at that ball, now. Hit it! Let's go!"

The first Laser up was Brenda. Whoosh! The first pitch was *fast!*

"Steeeeerike!"

The second pitch smacked into the catcher's mitt.

"Steeeeerike two!"

"Come on, Brenda!" shouted Mr. Slith. "Get mad at it!"

Brenda gritted her teeth. Her eyes grew wide. She shuffled her feet. And when the pitcher let the ball fly, she screamed "Yaaaaaahhhhhhh!" and took a huge swing.

Crack! A line drive to center. Base hit. The Lasers went crazy.

The next two Laser batters, Curtis and Gene, struck out. Then, Marybeth hit one over the first baseman's head. Now the Lasers had Brenda on second and Marybeth on first. Flash stepped up to the plate.

"Let's go, Flash!" everybody on the bench and along the sidelines yelled.

The pitch came whizzing in and Flash took a big cut. *Whack!* It was a towering high fly to right field. The right fielder mover left, moved right, moved back, put up his glove, and...dropped it! The Lasers went crazy! Now there were bases loaded with two outs!

And I was up.

"Hey, the dog's up!" shouted one of the Tornadoes. "What a break! How can a dumb dog hit?"

Good question, I thought. Actually, I could just pick the bat up in my powerful jaws and swing it. But if I did, everybody there would probably be so terrified they would run away screaming. No, somehow I had to get a hit but still look like a fairly average dog.

"Time out!" Flash hollered from first. He trotted down the baseline and over to me. He grabbed my collar. "Come on, boy." He led me up to the batter's box. Then he placed a bat on the ground in front of me. "Stay, boy. Stay."

The Lucky Laundry Tornadoes were rolling on the ground laughing. Even most of the fans were giggling behind their hands. Then the Tornadoes' coach came out to the ump.

124

"Hey, ump, where's the strike zone on a dog? Two inches off the ground?"

"Good question," said the ump. "Well, no, that wouldn't be fair to the pitcher. I say anything above the dog's head is a ball, that okay with you?"

"Sure, why not," said the coach. He told his pitcher and ran off the field laughing.

"Strangest game I ever umpired," said the ump. "Play ball!"

Flash was back, leading off first base and yelling to me. "Pick up the bat, boy. Pick up the bat!"

That brought a new wave of laughter.

Me, I was cool. I stood there in the batter's box and blinked my eyes and panted and smiled as Flash talked to me from first. The fans loved it. I let two pitches go by. One strike, one ball.

"Come on, Scratch!" Flash called, getting desperate. "Bases loaded. Two out. You have to pick up the bat! Pick it up, boy!"

Oh, all right, I thought. I've kept them in enough suspense. The pitcher went into his windup, and just as he cocked his arm to throw, I lowered my head, grabbed the bat right in the center, and lifted it up so the head of the bat was over the plate. As the ball zoomed in, I angled the bat just right—of course, no one even suspected what I was doing. Then I raised the bat about an inch and a half...

Bonk. I bunted the ball and the ballpark exploded.

The fans and the Lasers cheered their brains out. Before Flash took off for second, he screamed, "Here, boy! Here, boy! Here, boy!" He was trying to get me to run to first. So I did. The fans went bonkers.

Meanwhile, the ball was dribbling down the third-base line, just where I had aimed it to go. All the base runners were running. Brenda was churning hard toward home plate. The pitcher was racing for the ball, and when he got to it, Brenda was about three steps from home.

The pitcher threw the ball. The catcher reached out to grab it. Brenda's feet flew forward and she skidded into a huge, dusty slide toward home plate. The ball smacked into the catcher's mitt and the catcher yanked it down for the tag. Brenda's foot slid along the ground, right between the catcher's legs toward home. The dust billowed up around them as Brenda crashed into the catcher, who buckled and tumbled down on top of her. The umpire flung out his arms.

"SAFE!"

The crowd erupted with cheers. Mr. Slith called time out as the Lasers danced and yelled and ran out to Brenda. The Tornadoes scratched their heads. Me, I was standing calmly on first base. The hero. It was nothing really—only the greatest moment in my whole life! I looked over to Kong, and he was racing up and down the sidelines, barking and jumping around. Flash, in fact, was doing the same thing.

And then I saw someone else calmly sitting beside her master. Marzipan! My heart started thumping. The beautiful dog I loved had seen my greatest moment! She smiled at me and flapped me a kiss with her tongue. I wanted to faint. I wanted to cheer. I wanted to lift my leg really bad. Oh, boy! What a day!

Finally, the umpire ordered everybody back to

the benches and the next batter came up to the plate. It was quiet George, our catcher. On the first pitch, he grounded out to third base. But we were ahead, 1 to 0!

Before the Lasers went back out onto the field, Mr. Slith gathered us around for a pep talk. "Now we have to keep mean out there. Have to keep thinking. Have to...holy cow!"

There, standing all alone at the end of the bench, was Brick Glick. No one could do anything for a second but stare.

"I..." he said. "I feel better now."

"You what?" said Mr. Slith.

"I'm okay now, I'm not sick anymore. And I'm sorry. I want to play baseball."

"You do?" said most of the Lasers.

"Yeah, I do," he said. "I've been very unprofessional and I want to make up for it. I'm not asking you to forgive me for stealing Rosie's cats. All I want right now is for you to let me play. Please?"

"Well, team," said Mr. Slith, "what do you say? It's up to you."

Rosie walked up to Brick and held out her hand. "You're the best center fielder around, and sure you can play. We always wanted you to play. It was you who didn't."

"Gee, I—" began Brick.

"And I forgive you for stealing my cats," said Rosie. "I know how you must feel being on a team that isn't so hot. I've been through something like it. I was in this play at school and everybody but me kept forgetting their lines. I knew that when we put on the show I would be embarrassed in front of my parents and everybody. So, I wanted to just quit. See, the play was about this princess who—"

128

"Um, Rosie?" Flash said. "Mind if the rest of us say something?"

Rosie blushed. "Sorry. I just... well, you know."

"Sure," said Flash. "Brick, we all want you back on the team. Come on, let's play the game of our lives."

"Okay!" said Brick, beaming.

"Let's go, Lasers!" called the ump.

"Got a substitution," Mr. Slith called back. "Brick Glick for Scratch."

"Brick Glick," one of the Tornadoes said. "Oh, no!"

"Come on, Lasers!" yelled Flash. "Let's hit the field!" Then Flash leaned down to me. "Scratch, sorry, boy. You did great, really great!"

All my other teammates patted me as they went out onto the field. I was proud of myself. I did my job. I was a pro.

On the way out to the field, Brick said to the team, "So why didn't you guys score more runs, huh?"

"What?" they said.

"Yeah," Brick said. "If you were really professional, you would have tried a squeeze play when George was up, and—"

Flash let loose with a laugh. "Welcome back, Brick!"

The game went on, and it was a good one, too. Rosie's pitching was terrific, and the Tornadoes buckled down and played great. But Brick—well, he was excellent. He raced around center field catching everything. He even caught a fly ball to right field that had bounced off Gene's glove. Brick dove and caught it before it hit the ground! It was the best catch I'd ever seen.

The tension built until the last inning. It was the top of the ninth and the Tornadoes had bases loaded with two outs. And their best slugger was at the plate with a full count. If Rosie walked him, the Tornadoes would score.

Rosie got this wild look in her eye. She wound up, cocked her arm, and threw the fastest bullet of the game.

"Steeeeeerike three! Game over! Lasers win, one to nothing!"

We had beaten the undefeated, first-place, best team in the league—maybe in the whole world.

The fans on the sidelines burst into cheers and jumped up and down. Kong howled like mad. All the Lasers threw their pink caps in the air and twirled and screamed and ran up and mobbed Rosie, then patted Mr. Slith on the back until he fell down. Then they shook hands with the sad and shocked Tornadoes.

And then all the Lasers turned together and ran straight toward me.

Flash grabbed me around my neck and gave me a huge hug. Someone else grabbed my back legs. And while a hundred hands patted me all over, I was hoisted way up in the air onto the top of shoulders and carried around.

"The hero! The hero!" they yelled. "Scratch is the hero of the game!"

Wow, what a feeling! They turned and carried me out toward the parking lot. Marzipan and I exchanged winks as I passed. Then I saw Miss Bliss running up to Rosie.

"Congratulations, Rosie!" said Miss Bliss.

"Thanks!" she said.

"And I have some very good news!" said Miss

Bliss. "Your mother has agreed to let me adopt your Three Stooges! Isn't that wonderful!"

The whole team shouted: "Yay!"

Everybody piled into a few cars, and I rode on Flash's lap to Joe's Pizza Parlor, where the whole team, including me, pigged out on pizza and root beers.

And everybody couldn't stop talking about the legendary bunt that Scratch the Pink Bunny Laser had laid down to win the biggest game in the world.

Fourteen: Little Scratches

Monday morning the newspaper came out. The fat man at *The News* had rewritten the lost cats article with a new headline that read: KID DETECTIVE, FLASH FRY, CRACKS KITTY CASE! The story went on to say how Flash found Rosie's cats and Mrs. Wain's cats on the same day. But the story mentioned nothing about how Brick had snatched them. All of us had decided to keep that a secret, because Brick had learned his lesson.

And in the sports section of the newspaper was a long article with the headline: DOG STARS IN LASERS SURPRISE UPSET WIN OVER FIRST-PLACE TORNADOES.

"Yup," Flash Fry was saying into his tape recorder with twenty-five copies of *The News* piled on his desk, "it was quite a day for both Flash Fry, Private Eye, and Scratch, Private Nose and Base-

133

ball Star. Come to think of it, I wouldn't have solved this complex and baffling cat case without Scratch, *and* our team wouldn't have won the game without him either. No detective in the world has a better partner, or a better friend." He shut off the tape recorder to give me a big hug.

I sure do love my boy.

Speaking of love, I got some really terrific news about two months later. Marzipan had eight adorable puppies. I suddenly had three sons and five daughters! And, naturally, they were all handsome pups, too! They were on the short, muscular side like me, but they had Marzipan's beautiful red hair. I was so proud! And I plan on spending a lot of time with them so I can teach them everything I know about detective work—and baseball—because now I've got a whole team of my own!